Seven Daze

Low-Rent Rendezvous
Book Seven in the Val Fremden Midlife Mystery Series
Margaret Lashley

This book is a work of fiction. While actual places throughout Florida have been used in this book, any resemblance to persons living or dead are purely coincidental. Unless otherwise noted, the author and the publisher make no explicit guarantees as to the accuracy of the information contained in this book and in some cases, the names of places have been altered.

What Readers are Saying about the Val Fremden Midlife Mystery Series

"Hooked like a fish. OMG Margaret Lashley is the best! Val could be Stephanie Plum's double!! Phenomenal writing."

"I love this rollicking series. Hilarious, exceedingly well crafted, amazingly quirky characters."

"The characters and interaction in this book are totally 'wet your pants laughing' funny!! Don't believe me? Grab a copy for yourself and see."

"I was totally surprised, after many twists and false clues, by the ultimate killer...."

"I like mysteries that, like I found this one, are not easily solved, And Val's constant run-ins with the local police and her fellow campers are crazy, humorous, or both."

"Totally madcap and zany."

"I loved this book! It was still hysterically funny."

"If you enjoy Janet Evanovich you will love Margaret Lashley!"

More Hilarious Val Fremden Midlife Mysteries

by Margaret Lashley
Absolute Zero
Glad One
Two Crazy
Three Dumb
What Four
Five Oh
Six Tricks
Seven Daze
Figure Eight
Cloud Nine

"THERE'S ALL KINDS OF okay in this world. And I'm okay with that."

Val Fremden

Chapter One

I thought seven was supposed to be a lucky number. Maybe it was...for *dwarves*.

But *me?* Not so much.

In fact, every time that number popped up in my life, I gave it a little side-eye. Seven wasn't lucky. It was a boil on my buttocks. An ugly reminder of how close I'd come to living in a cardboard box, wrestling alley cats for empty tuna cans.

A few years back, before I returned to Florida, I'd spent seven years in Germany. That's when I found out that seven years abroad was exactly how long it took to destroy my life savings *and* my life in general. I'd washed up back on the shores of my hometown, St. Pete Beach, not just broke and homeless. I'd also been pretty much erased from the hearts, minds and credit histories of every person and place I'd ever thought I could count on.

Geez.

Even my *name* had become a stranger. Literally. The old Val Jolly I'd been before I left for Europe was gone. A bad marriage had changed it to Val *Fremden*—a word that meant "stranger" in German. It's almost scary to think how apropos *that* had turned out to be....

So screw you, seven.

Come to think of it, six was no good, either. It reminded me of what a magnet for mayhem I could be. Six times now, I've ended up smack-dab in the middle of a nut-fest of squirrelly shenanigans no sane person could have imagined. Like hobgoblins inhabiting an unsound mind, bulldog-faced bullies, shady shysters, fruitcake relatives and nutty neighbors seemed to track me down and stick to me like Crazy Glue.

Don't even get me started on five. It was the number of years I've had to lick my wounds since I got torpedoed by a German dreamboat.

Anchors away, dirtbag.

Four wasn't much better. That was how many times I've had to start my life over. *With nothing*.

As far as three went...well, that was the number of times I'd been married. Or, perhaps more accurately, it was the number of times I'd been *divorced*.

Over the years, I'd become deeply suspicious of the numeral two, as well. Two was a pair. A matched set. If you don't get my drift, go back and read number three.

I never have understood eight, either. To me, it always looked like an infinity symbol that had been stood on its head. No thanks. My life didn't need any more help going off-kilter.

And nine? Nine sounded like German for "no." A non-starter on both counts.

Nope. In my book, the luckiest number was one. *Numero uno.* As in me, myself and I. During my extended tutelage at the School of Hard Knocks, I'd learned that *one* was the single digit I could consistently rely on.

Even if it was odd.

JUST WHEN I THOUGHT everything in my life had returned to a semblance of normalcy, I opened the mailbox and screamed. Inside was a letter from the AARP. It was official. The world had just declared me "old."

"You all right over there?"

I glanced over my left shoulder. My neighbor, Laverne Cowens, was waving at me from the other side of her mailbox.

In the full light of day, the radiant glare rocketing off her gold-lame jumpsuit nearly blinded me. Either that, or I'd succumbed to cataracts. I squinted and waved the letter back at her.

"Ugh! Laverne, I've just been 'AARPed.'"

"Oh," she grinned and shook her horsey head. "That ain't nothin'. Wait 'til you get your first coupons for Depends. *Then* we've got something to talk about."

My upper lip snarled involuntarily.

"Can't wait."

I turned toward the house, then changed my mind. I was stalling. I knew it, but I didn't care. Anything was better than going back inside to face "it."

Up to now, I'd made a point of trying to steer clear of Laverne's personal life, but I was out of ideas and just desperate enough to push the scales in her favor. I forced a smile.

"Hey Laverne, how are things going with you and J.D.?"

At the mention of her boyfriend's name, Laverne's grin faded like a cheap tattoo.

"We haven't killed each other yet, so there's that," she joked half-heartedly. One of her penciled-on eyebrows jerked upward. "How about you? I noticed a bunch of moving boxes going into your house yesterday."

"Yeah," I sighed as I made my way along the sidewalk toward her. "Tom's almost moved in."

"Boy howdy. He's not wasting any time, is he?"

"No."

I blew out a breath. "I guess it's like lancing a boil. Better to just dig in and get it over with."

Laverne's red lips twisted into a smirk. "How romantic."

I shook my head. "Sorry. Sometimes, I really think I should just be taken out and shot."

Laverne snorted, giving me a gander at her dentures.

"We can't all be hopeless romantics now, can we?"

"No, I suppose not. But why is it I only ever seem to get the 'hopeless' part down pat?"

"Ha ha!" she laughed. "Honey, you always know how to make me laugh. Want to come in for a drink?"

"It's ten-thirty in the morning, Laverne."

Laverne shrugged. "So?"

I glanced around at the neighbors' houses. Nobody was around.

"Okay. What the heck."

I FOLLOWED THE SKINNY old woman up her driveway toward her modest, ranch-style house. Built in the 1950s, it was a mirror image of my own little abode. If our homes hadn't butted up to the Intracoastal Waterway leading out to the Gulf of Mexico, most people wouldn't have given the low-slung, concrete-block boxes a second glance. In fact, nowadays, the only reason anyone bought a place like ours was to doze it and build a McMansion on the lot.

But folks like Laverne and me preferred character over modern conveniences. At least that's the story I told myself. I didn't have enough money to remodel my vintage kitchen, much less rebuild the whole house. And I kind of liked that my place had a "lived in" appearance. The delicate pallor of impending poverty came in handy. It kept away would-be door-to-door solicitors and Halloween trick-or-treaters.

On the outside, Laverne's place was just like mine. It was a tad faded, and as non-descript as an out-of-shape, ball-capped man at a sports bar. But *inside?* Now, *that* was a different story.

Amongst the hallowed rooms of Laverne's lair lurked the biggest collection of Vegas memorabilia outside Madame Tussauds' wax museum in Las Vegas proper. As I followed her inside the door and waded past bookshelves cluttered with tacky souvenirs, I noticed that something was off. Laverne's living room, once an unabridged shrine to all things happy, glitzy and glittery, had been infiltrated by an army of somber, humorless invaders.

On the wall beside the stunning, life-sized, color photo of Laverne in her feathery cabaret outfit being kissed on the cheek by Elvis, hung a black-and-white picture of a dour group of short, angry-looking men dressed in lederhosen. Their expressions seemed to convey they were recent graduates of the Sauerkraut Club. Laverne's bookcase, once chock-a-block with shiny celebrity figurines like a mini Oscar-Awards after-party, now had dull-hued, kerchief-wearing Hummel figures milling about in the crowd like babushka-headed party poopers.

I shot a worried glance at Laverne as she pulled a couple of beers from her fridge. "How far has J.D. gotten with this?" I asked.

"With what?" she asked.

"This...I dunno...*hostile takeover* of your space."

"You noticed, huh?" Laverne shook her head. "Sheesh. He wants me to drink beer out of a stein, Val. A *stein!* I got my doubts, honey. I'm not so sure it's gonna work out with us."

"Why? I *know* you like beer."

"Sure. But I only drink it out of the bottle...or my lucky Marilyn Monroe leg."

Laverne opened a kitchen cabinet and pulled out a flesh-colored, leg-shaped glass complete with white high-heel and fishnet stocking.

"I don't do steins," she muttered. "And I'm beginning to think I don't do roommates, either."

"Oh." I slumped on my stool. "Sorry to hear that. Well, I guess it's good you two didn't tie the knot. At least you and J.D. can dial back the living-together thing pretty easily, right?"

Laverne cracked open a can of beer and began to fill the shapely leg with golden liquid and foam.

"I guess. I mean, he's still got his place on the beach and all."

My chin met my neck.

"J.D.'s got a house on the beach?"

"Yeah. Sunset Beach," Laverne said, and sulked at the leg, as if it might've been Marilyn's fault.

I glanced around with fresh eyes at the garish clutter crammed in every crevice of Laverne's kitchen. A bobble-headed Dean Martin winked at me.

"And J.D. chose to live *here* instead? Why?"

"Beats me," Laverne answered. She shoved a shamrock-covered glass full of beer across the counter toward me. "Because *I'm* here, I guess. And because I don't want to live on the beach."

I couldn't have been more incredulous if Laverne had just confessed she wanted to live in a dumpster with Frosty the Snowman.

"Why not?"

"Because *this* is my home, Val."

Laverne looked around her place with sad, puppy-dog eyes. "And *you're* next door. I like having you nearby. I don't feel like I'm all alone."

Laverne's words tapped a nerve. Hard. Like a spike hammered into a beer keg.

The fact that J.D.'s memorabilia had distinctly German roots reminded me of all the lonely, soul-sucking years I'd spent in Germany, forlorn and friendless. My heart flinched at the rush of painful memories—of feeling hollowed out, vulnerable and fragile. Then I realized, to my great relief, that I hadn't felt that way in a long, long time.

My gut instinct was to warn Laverne. But of what? Geez, given my track record, I was in no position to give relationship advice.

"Compromise is hard," I offered, trying to put a positive spin on the personal dread that had begun to churn like sour milk in my stomach. "But, you know, it's not like you'd be moving to another *country* or something. Sunset Beach is only a few minutes' drive from here."

"True. But it's not *here*."

Laverne pouted and stared at me with her endearing pug eyes. "I know it sounds corny, but home is where your *heart* is, Val. And my heart's *right here*."

My eyes began to sting. "Then *here* is where you should stay. After all, it's *your* life." I sniffed back a totally unexpected tear.

Was I getting sentimental in my old age, or just going senile? What next? Crying at dog food commercials?

I grabbed my glass. "Hey, how about a toast?"

"To what?"

"To knowing where your home is."

Laverne grinned. "To knowing home when you see it." She hoisted Marilyn's leg.

I sipped my beer and watched the old woman take a long, throat-bobbing chug. Her grin returned. She set the leg-mug down on the counter and asked, "You got any super glue?"

I nearly spewed my beer. "What?"

Laverne opened a drawer and pulled out a baggie containing the shattered remains of what appeared to have once been a Hummel figurine.

"I...uh...accidently dropped this."

I stifled a smirk.

"I don't have any more glue, Laverne. I used it all up fixing Tom's acrylic baseball case. I...uh...accidently dropped *it* yesterday."

We eyed each other and burst out laughing.

"It would appear that great minds think alike," I said, and drained the beer from my Shamrock Casino glass as Laverne wiped the corners of her eyes with a paper towel.

"Thanks, honey. I needed a good laugh."

"We both did," I said. "Boyfriend business can be tough."

I set my empty glass on the counter and looked around her place again. "I'm curious, Laverne. What exactly do you *do* all day?"

Laverne shrugged nonchalantly. "Whatever I want."

I nodded appreciatively. "You don't say."

Laverne picked up Marilyn's leg and finished off her beer, blissfully unaware that she looked like the femme fatal in a flesh-eating zombie spoof. She set the empty leg on the counter and grinned at me.

"So, how's the writing going?"

My smirk faded. "Slow. I'm still setting up my writing space in the second bedroom."

"Give it time, honey."

I blew out a sigh. "You're right. I shouldn't press myself. Now that Tom's living with me, he's helping out with the bills. I hope that'll take the pressure off my savings account."

"I heard that."

Laverne stepped over to the sink to give Marilyn's leg a rinse. The sight of a fishnet-clad shin in the drain-board was unsettling enough. But the faded Vegas showgirl upped the ante by sliding a plate of cookies across the counter at me.

"Want one? Snickerdoodles. I made them in cooking class."

I'd never been startled by a cookie before—not even one of Laverne's. I eyed the misshapen, hideous globs of dough. Pale, gooey middles surrounded by charred edges. They reminded me of petrified splats of vomit—with eyeballs in them.

I thought about Laverne's boyfriend, J.D., who faced culinary trials like this one on a daily basis. I wished I'd had one of his baggies tucked in my waistband so I could fake eating the cookie, smuggle out its remains, and dispose of it in a toxic waste container.

"I'm on a diet," I lied.

"Suit yourself." Laverne picked up a cookie.

"Wait a minute. I thought you got banned from cooking classes at the senior center."

Laverne shrugged. "You set one little oven on fire and you're black-balled for life. I'm telling you, Val, those old folks got no sense of humor."

She poked the horrid cookie at me as if to prove her point. My body shrunk back involuntarily.

"Nope. This new class is down at St. Pete College. Continuing ed."

Laverne put down the cookie and picked up a brochure. She reached a long, skinny arm across the counter and handed it to me. "See? They've got all kinds of classes. And the best thing is, not everybody there's got a blue rinse in their hair and a stick up their butt."

I glanced through the brochure.

"Huh. It says here they have a writer's class. *Mystery Writing for Fun and Profit*. Meets Thursday nights from six to eight."

"That's tomorrow!" Laverne squealed. "Same time as my cooking class!"

"But it started last week," I muttered.

"So? You've only missed one class. Why don't you take it? We can ride over together. It'll be fun!"

"I dunno."

"What have you got to lose? And Val, it's in the *evening*. Think about it. That's free time *away from the guys*." She jabbed a red-lacquered nail at the brochure. "And like it says here, you can 'Explore Your Inner Aptitudes.'"

"Or *inept*itudes."

I bit my lip and read the brief syllabus while Laverne drummed her nails on the counter.

"Val, thirty-five bucks buys seven weeks of 'Thursday evening, do-as-you-damn-well-please' time."

I looked up at Laverne with a new admiration.

"Excellent point, my friend. Mind if I use your phone?"

Chapter Two

Ever since I'd quit my job at Griffith & Maas last week, I'd been living a lie.

I'd bought a new laptop and a cheap acrylic desk. I'd set up the second bedroom as a makeshift office. I was going to be a writer again.

But I wasn't writing.

I'd spent Monday sitting at my desk staring at my laptop and playing solitaire. Tuesday I'd stared at my laptop and used an old toothbrush to clean every inch of grout in the bathroom. Yesterday, I'd organized the junk drawer and sorted rubber bands and paperclips by size and color. Today I'd cleaned out the refrigerator by eating all the leftovers—including ketchup packets and every olive and pickle unfortunate enough to be apprehended while swimming around innocently in a jar full of brine.

I was supposed to be *writing*. But the words wouldn't come. What kind of story did *I* have to tell, anyway? How to arrange dryer lint into fun animal shapes?

It had been weird enough not going to work anymore. Every morning this week I'd peered through the front blinds as Tom had driven away in his SUV. I knew that after he kissed me goodbye and headed to his job, I was free to write. But I hadn't *felt* free. Instead of using my imagination for writing novels, I'd used it to put bars on the windows and roadblocks in my brain.

I'd become my own jailer. And my sentence was *to write sentences!*

It was too much pressure. Getting that blasted AARP notice yesterday hadn't helped, either. For me, it hadn't been an anonymous, over-fifty rite of passage. It had been a very *personal* wake-up call; A "Come on down!" shout-out from the MC in the gameshow called *My Life*.

I was running out of time to do something big with my time on Earth. Writing might be my last chance...and what was I doing with it? I was blowing it! Instead of cranking out stories, I was hurtling down a slippery slope on a pair of thighs that proved beyond a shadow of a doubt that gravity was no longer my friend.

I stared at the blank laptop screen as if it might rescue me from myself. It stared back, not offering even so much as a pity blink. I put my head in my hands.

What am I doing? I don't have any more time to waste! I need to write the next great American novel before dementia sets in!

But the black void of the computer screen wasn't about to divulge its secret plots today. And for some reason, no amount of internal prodding, pleading, or psychotic, blackmail-type threats could motivate my mind, or get my fingers to press the keys. Anything and *everything* seemed more appealing than writing.

Even scrubbing the toilet.

My worst nemesis was the fridge. As I sat at my desk, the evil food in the refrigerator called to me like a siren's song, luring me to my death by morbid obesity.

As I scraped the last of the peanut butter out of the jar, I hoped the mystery writing class tonight would give me some inspiration. If not, my only memorable life accomplishment might turn out to be that when I die, I'll have to be hauled from my house with a forklift and buried in a piano case.

"WHAT DID YOU DO TODAY?" Laverne asked as she climbed in-to Shabby Maggie, my 1963 Ford Falcon Sprint convertible.

My back bristled.

"Don't ask. Hey, do you know how to get mustard stains out of up-holstery?"

"No. But I know how to get blood stains out of cotton sheets."

I eyed the old woman. She was wearing a putrid green pantsuit. "Don't tell me. Vegas days?"

"Yep."

I smiled. "I bet your life would make a good novel, Laverne."

"Sure, kid," she shrugged. "Anyone's would. So, how's your book coming along?"

A hot flash of desperation shot through me. Either that or I'd gone menopausal.

"Not so great. Working from home is harder than I thought. I need...*inspiration*."

Laverne's head jerked to the right. Her eyes bugged out like a car-toon character who'd just spotted an oncoming bus. I followed her line of sight. J.D.'s white Mercedes was pulling up in her driveway.

Laverne nudged me on the shoulder. "Step on it, Val, or we'll be late for class."

"Trouble in paradise?" I asked.

Laverne looked me up and down and smiled brightly. "Yeah, honey. That would be a great name for your novel!"

"MY NAME IS ANGELA LANGSBURY," the scrawny, silver-haired woman at the front of the classroom said as I walked in. She was pencil thin. Blue veins ran up her forearms and temples like worms under the surface of milky Jell-O. She wore a faded, black, sack of a dress and leaned on the edge of a metal desk in a narrow, angular room the color of a grey whale's posterior.

Five desks, four of which were already occupied, faced the teacher. A blackboard covered most of the wall behind her.

I snickered and made my way toward the last open seat.

"Excuse me," Ms. Langsbury said. "I don't see what's so funny...Miss?"

"Val Fremden," I answered. "Sorry. I thought you were making a joke. Angela Lansbury? As in *Murder She*—"

"I get it," Langsbury said in a tone that implied she'd heard it all before about a trillion times. Her black, beady eyes bore through mine until I shrunk two inches. I took another hesitant step toward the empty desk.

"Ms. Fremden, please remain standing," Langsbury said. Her voice sounded like nails on a chalkboard. My spine arched. "Class. What can you tell me about the woman who just entered the room?"

My face grew hot as I stood and tried not to meet eyes with my jury. It was a lineup of three middle-aged women of various shapes and sizes, and one young guy with a soul patch whose expression made me suspect he just might have been there against his will.

"She's late," said a woman with ugly librarian glasses and a face to match.

"What else?" Langsbury asked, and looked me over as if I were an art-class model.

"She's disrespectful," said another woman with red hair and a pinched expression.

"She's got a weird sense of humor," said a familiar voice. I dared a glance her way. There sat Judy Bloomers, a real estate agent I'd met a few weeks back.

"Her jeans are too tight," said the young man.

The room went silent. The glowering looks he got from me and the other women caused the hipster-wannabe to shrivel even further behind his desk.

"Okay. Enough," said Langsbury. "I see some of you remembered last week's lesson and stuck to the facts without interpretation. Victoria, you're right. She is, indeed, late."

The library-faced lady sneered at me smugly.

"Disrespectful?" Langsbury continued. "Yes, she's expressed this tendency with both tardiness and rudeness. Good observation, Clarice."

The red-haired lady crinkled her thin nose and smiled as if it pained her to do so.

"Jeff, you said her jeans were too tight," Langsbury said. "This is a highly subjective comment. I suppose, in some country, *somewhere*, jeans that tight could be considered appropriate." She glanced at me and smirked almost imperceptibly.

"And Judy, the comment about the weird sense of humor is yet to be determined. It will require more observation. Thank you, Ms. Flintstone. You can take your seat now."

"It's Fremden," I corrected.

"Of course," said Langsbury. "So, we are agreed, then? Names are no laughing matter."

I bit my lip. "Agreed."

The class laughed nervously as I slid into the last open chair. My face burned with embarrassment and anger.

How rude!

As soon as my butt hit the chair, I lifted it again.

I don't need this crap! I'm leaving!

My butt was hovering midway off the seat when what Langsbury said next made me set it back down again.

"Ms. Fremden," she asked, "what's the cardinal rule for writing a good novel?"

How should I know? That's why I'm here, Sherlock!

I didn't want to add "stupid" to my rapidly growing list of undesirable attributes, so I scanned my brain and came up with something I'd heard somewhere before.

"Uh...write what you know?"

"If that were true, there wouldn't be any science fiction novels, now would there?" Langsbury said.

"Uh...no," I admitted.

"Or romance novels either," Judy quipped. "Think about it. I'd believe in Martians faster than I'd believe in a guy with ripped abs that swept me off my feet, then swept the floor and washed the dishes."

The whole class laughed, including Langsbury.

"Judy's right," Langsbury said. "Write what you know and you'll bore yourself *and* your readers to tears. No. The correct answer is to write what you're *curious* about. Write about what *excites* you. So, tell us, Ms. Fremden. What would get you excited?"

"Uh...a sale on magic jeans that made your butt three sizes smaller?"

Ms. Langsbury smiled. "The Case of the Magic Jeans. It has a nice ring to it for a mystery. Don't you agree, class?"

I glanced around the room. All smiles. Langsbury winked at me.

And just like that, I'd been redeemed.

MS. LANSGBURY SPENT the next two hours reviewing the "dos and don'ts" of writing mysteries. How to develop characters and story lines. How to avoid plotting yourself into a corner. And, of course, how to dodge the dreaded ending everyone saw coming.

Geez! There was so much more to writing novels than I'd thought. By the end of the class, my head was spinning. Two hours had flown by.

"All right, class, that's it," Langsbury said.

She tapped a piece of chalk on the board and wrote out the words, 'Five Unique Ways to Kill Someone.'

"This week's homework assignment is to imagine how you might be able to get away with murder," she said. "Next Thursday, I want to see a short story and a list of five original ways to help someone bite the dust."

"Who should we kill?" asked Victoria, the woman impersonating a snooty librarian.

"Anyone," Langsbury answered. "A coworker. Family member. Spouse."

"I don't need any more ideas on how to get rid of a husband," Judy sneered. "I've got a list as long as my arm. I was married for twenty-eight years, after all."

The women laughed appreciatively. Jeff looked as if he were counting the number of steps to the exit door.

"Oh! One final thing," Langsbury said as we rose from our seats. "Don't forget about the writer's retreat coming up in Orlando. I'll need to know next week for sure who's coming. And you'll need to pay your five-hundred dollar deposit to secure a spot."

"I missed last week," I said to Langsbury as the others filed out of the room. "What's this writer's retreat about?"

"It's akin to a murder-mystery weekend," she explained. "We spend three days at a bed and breakfast outside Altamonte Springs. I give vague details about a recent murder, and have various characters drop by for lunch and drinks. Participants have to study them, interview them, and ultimately try to determine who the murderer was based on the clues and evidence presented."

"Sounds like a typical weekend at my relatives," Judy quipped.

Langsbury shot Judy some side-eye and poked a piece of paper at me. "Here's a flyer if you're interested."

"Thanks," I said, and walked out with Judy.

I glanced at the flyer. "Geez! Eighteen hundred bucks for a weekend of pretending to be Agatha Christie? That's pretty steep."

"Yeah," Judy agreed. "Too rich for my blood."

"So, what are you doing here?" I asked. "Do you want to write mystery novels?"

Judy smirked. "Wow, Val. Your powers of deduction are astounding."

I punched her on the arm. "Ha ha."

Judy shrugged. "I dunno. I've thought about it off and on my whole life. I heard about this class and figured, why not give it a go."

"I used to be a copy writer," I muttered. "Everybody thinks they can write a book."

"I'm a real estate agent," Judy sneered. "Everybody thinks they can sell a house."

I winced. "Sorry. I didn't mean to insult you."

"Don't worry about it," Judy shrugged. "I've got thick skin. But hey, I've gotta know. How's it working out with your new neighbor? The guy who barbequed his mother?"

"He didn't barbeque.... Look, come to find out, he's actually a nice guy. And it turns out that spontaneous human combustion is a real thing."

"Really?" Judy kicked a stone off the sidewalk. "Too bad. I was going to use that as one of my five ways to knock somebody off."

"Why? I thought you had a string of ideas as long as your arm."

"I'm in sales. We have a tendency to, shall I say, *enhance assets*."

"Oh." I grinned and swished my bottom. "Kind of like how my jeans enhance mine?"

Judy laughed. "Well, I don't think I would stretch the truth *that* far."

Chapter Three

"Wasn't that the real estate lady?" Laverne asked as she angled her stork legs into Maggie's passenger seat. In the moonlight, dressed in a light-green pantsuit, she looked like a trans-gender cicada.

"Yeah. Judy Bloomers. Turns out she's interested in writing novels, too."

"Like I said, everybody's life's a book, Val. Only difference is, some books are more open than others."

"That's rather philosophical of you, Laverne. What brought that on?"

"I dunno. I guess I just can't figure out how my own story ends."

"What do you mean?"

Laverne's shoulders heaved as she let out a huge sigh. "There's no other way to say it, Val. I just can't picture me growing old with J.D."

I gave Laverne a tight smile. "I can't picture you growing old, period," I said. "You're too full of life."

Laverne smiled. "Thanks, sugar."

"What's J.D. done? Besides invade your territory, I mean."

"Nothing, really," Laverne confessed. "It's more what he *hasn't* done. Or maybe what he *doesn't* do. I dunno, Val. It's hard to explain. J.D. doesn't like my Vegas stuff. And he hates my cooking. He thinks my clothes aren't proper, either. He bought me this pantsuit, you know. Is it just me, or do I look like a lizard's grandma?"

I winced.

"Well?" Laverne asked. "What do you think?"

I stared into Laverne's watery eyes.

"Since you're asking, Laverne, I think any man who doesn't appreciate you just the way you are has got no taste at all."

"WHY ARE YOU LOOKING at me funny?" Tom asked from his perch on a barstool at my kitchen counter. "Is there something in my hair?"

He ran a hand through his blond bangs and studied me with his twinkling, sea-green eyes.

"Oh, no reason," I said, and sucked in a breath. He'd caught me staring at him absently, imagining a noose around his neck. "Sorry. I was just thinking about the assignment from my writing class."

Tom rolled a crisp, white sleeve up his tan, muscled forearm. "So, what's the assignment?"

"Uh...I've got to think of five unique ways to kill someone."

Tom's eyebrows rose slightly. "I see." He smirked. "Anything you want to tell me?"

"What do you mean?" I asked, my voice wavering between guilt and innocence.

Tom looked down at his beer for a moment. "Me moving in. It's a big step, I know." His eyes flashed up at mine playfully. "You'd let me know if you were contemplating homicide, wouldn't you?"

I laughed awkwardly. "Don't be ridiculous!"

"I don't mind being ridiculous," he countered. "But I *do* mind being dead. If something's bothering you, let's talk about it—*before* things get out of hand."

"Okay."

"I want you to know, I'm looking at this as an experiment, Val. Me moving in, I mean. What's done can be undone. I can move out if it's too much. You don't have to resort to murder. I'm a policeman. I can take a hint."

"Thanks," I said, and swallowed a lump. "I'll admit, it's an adjustment. And there's something else...."

I took Tom's hand.

"Don't get this wrong. I've been thinking. I want...I want to put a daybed in my office. Just so I can have the option, you know, to sleep somewhere else."

Tom's worried face went slack. "I knew it. Me moving in is too much for you, isn't it?"

"No," I blurted, then backtracked. Tom was right. I needed to be honest if this was going to work. "I mean, maybe...all at once, yes. But Tom, there's really no other way to do it, is there?"

"Good thing I kept the moving boxes," Tom joked bitterly.

I squeezed his hand.

"I'm not saying I want you to leave, Tom. Not at all. It's just...well, with my other relationships, I always felt trapped. Backed into a corner, you know?"

Tom looked at me, the sparkle gone from his eyes. "How is *our* situation any different? I honestly don't know how to make it work for you, Val."

My heart flinched.

"I think I felt trapped *before* because I didn't have any...*options*. Having this daybed thing...I don't know if I'll ever even *use* it, Tom. But it would be there. As an *option*. Don't you see?"

"No. Not really." Tom slumped over his barstool.

I got up and inched myself closer to him, until his inner thighs brushed against the sides of my waist. My hands squeezed his shoulders and I looked into his eyes.

"That way, every night when I climb into bed with you, it'll be a *choice*, Tom, not an *obligation*. Can you understand that? It's not that I don't want to be with you. I just don't want to have no option but to *have to* be with you."

I'd never seen Tom's face so dead serious.

"I get what this is all about," he said.

I gulped. "You do?"

Tom grinned and grabbed me around the waist. "You just want me to haul away that horrible guest bed, don't you?" He pulled me to him. "I'm nothing to you but a hunk of meat. Free labor. Muscle power."

I grinned through grateful tears and kissed him on the lips.

"Guilty as charged, officer."

I hugged him to me and whispered, "Thanks for getting it." I pulled away just enough to give him a lusty leer. "And, just so you know, I really *like* your muscle power."

Tom kissed me again, sending a jolt of electricity all the way to my knees. He brushed my hair from my eyes and whispered in my ear.

"Just so *you* know, I'm available right now. For a free demonstration. If you want, that is."

I grinned and kissed him hard on the lips.

"You know I never could resist a bargain."

"I'M STARVING," I SAID, and sat up in bed. The clock read 10:13 p.m. "With class and everything, I forgot to eat dinner. You want a baloney sandwich?"

Tom sat up on his elbow and grinned at me. "I thought you already served me one."

"Har har. I'm serious. The woman's name really *is* Angela Langsbury."

Tom shook his head. "I should have known. I gotta hand it to you, Val. Weird follows you wherever you go."

I smirked. "So I guess that means you're coming to the kitchen with me, then?"

Tom snorted with laughter. "I guess so."

He sat up in bed beside me. "Wanna know a secret?"

"Sure."

He nuzzled my neck. "I'd rather be weird with you than normal with anyone else."

I pushed him away. "Such a schmoozer. I knew there was *some* reason I kept you around."

I bit Tom lightly on the nose, then scampered out of his arms and down the hallway to the kitchen. I was slapping mustard on white bread when he ambled in, barefoot in boxers. I almost whistled. For a man his age, Tom still had it going on. Not quite a six-pack, but I never could handle more than three in a row.

"Got any pickles to go with that sandwich, ma'am?" he asked, and smoothed back his golden bangs.

I bit my lip. "Nope. Fresh out."

"You sure?"

"Absolutely, positively, without a shadow of a doubt."

"Okay, then. Glass of milk to go with it?"

"Coming right up."

I handed Tom a sandwich. He lifted the bread and inspected the baloney.

"What are you doing?" I asked.

Tom shot me a smirk. "I worked a homicide once where a woman put a foot-long piece of string in her husband's sandwich. He choked to death on it."

"Oh! That's good!" I plopped my sandwich onto the counter and ran toward my office.

"*Good?!*" Tom called after me. "Where are you going?"

"To write that down," I called back as I scribbled in my notepad. "And to put pickles on the grocery list!"

I wrote down "pickles" and padded back to the living room. "Want to make steaks for dinner tomorrow?"

"Can't." Tom took a bite of his sandwich. "We've got that thing at Winky's, remember?"

"Oh yeah," I muttered. "The cookout at the redneck corral."

Tom shook his head. "I still can't believe he got half a million bucks for Old Joe's Bait Shack."

"It'll be interesting to see what he's done with his windfall."

"Yeah. I bet *he's* not eating baloney tonight."

I grinned. "I wouldn't bet on it. So, Mister Detective, you got any more interesting ways to die you can tell me about?"

Tom smirked coyly. "Maybe. But it'll cost you."

"What?"

"How about a kiss per story."

"Wow," I said. "That sounds like a deal to me."

While we finished our sandwiches, Tom told me about a man who stabbed his partner with an icicle he'd fashioned in his freezer and carried with him in an Igloo cooler. The evidence had melted at the crime scene, but investigators were able to figure it out thanks to a bag of frozen cherries in the perp's freezer. They'd found cherry juice in the guy's fridge, in the cooler, and around the stab holes on the victim's shirt. Of course, I'd padded to my office and written it down in my notebook.

After our snack, as I brushed my teeth, I wondered about all the other ingenious methods people had devised over the centuries to do-in their partners.

The phrase, "The Kiss of Death" popped into my mind. I grinned, rinsed my mouth out, and applied a thick coat of imaginary, poison-laced lipstick.

I padded down the hall and climbed into bed next to Tom.

"Good night, dearest," I cooed, and planted a cyanide smacker on his lips.

Chapter Four

I grunted as I yanked the scratchy old sheets off the saggy, pee-stained mattress in my new office. It lay limp and stiff across the old box springs like a dead body.

At my request, Tom and one of his cop pals had hauled the dilapidated bed into the second bedroom last year. It had been my hope that its inhospitable lumps and pokey springs would ward away houseguests. But I'd found out the hard way that when you live near the beach, people were willing to put up with darn near anything for a free overnight stay.

"Are you sure you don't want me to haul this thing to the dump?" Tom asked.

He tapped a finger on the doorframe to my makeshift office. Fresh from the shower, he looked quite arresting in his crisply pressed police uniform.

"Nah. I'll order a daybed from Fred's Furniture. I'm pretty sure when they deliver it, they'll pick up the old mattress and dump it for free."

"Have it your way, murder-mystery gal," Tom quipped, and kissed me lightly on the lips.

He eyed the nasty mattress and crinkled his nose. "Just don't make me wake up dead with my body wrapped up in that thing like an old sausage roll."

I grinned. "A pig in a blanket? Way too obvious, Lieutenant."

Tom laughed. "Yeah. But you were thinking about it, weren't you?"

I rolled my eyes to one side. "I plead the Fifth."

Tom hugged me to his chest. "I'll let you off for bad behavior *this* time. But only because I've gotta go or I'll be late for work."

Tom kissed me goodbye at the front door. I waved, then watched through the blinds as he maneuvered his silver 4Runner down the driveway. I sighed and turned back to face the silent living room. I was alone again, with nothing for company but a blank computer screen and an empty fridge.

A tinge of panic shot through me. What was I going to do *now?*

I know! I can dust the ceiling! Yes, it's no good trying to write with dirty ceilings!

My brain was incorrigible.

I GRITTED MY TEETH and padded to the bathroom. As I reached for my toothbrush, I noticed Tom's hanging there beside mine in the black ceramic holder built into the wall. Its midnight-black hue was an odd, but rather interesting contrast to the rest of the flamingo-pink wall tiles. The 1950s must have been a pretty daring time—for color combinations, anyway.

Suddenly, a flashback, like a snippet of an old film, played before my eyes. It was a recollection of the very first time I'd seen this bathroom.

It had been almost four years ago to the day. It was summertime. The house had been closed up after my father Tony's death, and the place had been steamy-hot and claustrophobic. I was sticky and sweaty from clawing my way through a maze of heaped-up debris that had clogged the living room and hallway leading to the bathroom....

My skin pricked at the vivid memory.

I'd been wearing a sundress and sandals that day, but oh, how I'd wished I'd had on a hazmat suit. I snickered at the thought of Goober and Jorge rifling through the house along with me. I'd only known the guys for a few days back then, but I'd already learned enough about Winky to trust the other guys' instincts to leave him in the patrol car with Tom while we committed our unauthorized search of the place.

Oh, my gosh! Tom! That day was the very first time he'd ever met me!

I smiled. Fine, upstanding, irreproachable Lieutenant Thomas Foreman had been the picture of professionalism that day. Polite, but stoic. In conversation, he'd remained all business, despite the fact that, technically, he was aiding and abetting a break-in to help out his buddy Jorge.

And me.

Oh, geez! That day...I never really thought about it until now...but Tom...oh my word! He must have thought I was just some random, crazy woman committing a burglary with a bunch of hobos!

I shook my head. How in the world did the two of us ever get from *there* to *here*?

It had to have been some kind of freaking miracle.

I shook my head and stared at Tom's toothbrush hanging next to mine. A weird rush of Deja-vu swept over me. Again, I was transported back four years in time to the moment I'd discovered Glad's toothbrush hanging next to Tony's. It was then I'd realized there was more to her story than had first met the eye....

I opened the medicine cabinet, half expecting to see Glad's red lipstick and denture cream inside. But they weren't. Tom's razor and shaving cream had taken their place. They stared back at me, reminding me that everything had a way of coming back around full circle. Tom and I had replaced Tony and Glad...in this same space...just a different time.

Tom and I were a continuation of the age-old saga that had begun when the first pair of humans drew breath. We were just a man and a woman trying to find a way to make our lives work, *together*.

Glad had her Tony. I have my Tom.

I closed the medicine cabinet. "Tom is my Tony," I said to the woman staring back from the mirror.

And I hope he always will be.

In silent recognition of the wish I'd just made, I nodded at my reflection and switched off the light.

Now, I just need to figure out a way to kill him.

Or someone like him. For my class project, of course.

I padded back to my home office and plopped my butt in the desk chair. I turned on the computer, opened a file, and began to type.

Five Unique Ways to Kill Someone.

1) Icicle.

2) String in sandwich.

3) Poisoned lipstick.

4) Mattress roll-up.

5) Ty-D-Bol?

My stomach growled. I was out of pickles *and* ideas.

But at least I'd made a start.

WHAT DO YOU FEED A hungry redneck? I pondered as I wandered the aisles of Publix, my small, neighborhood, beach-themed grocery store.

I picked up a can of Vienna sausages and studied it.

What exactly are *"meat by-products" anyway?*

"Comparison shopping?" a familiar voice sounded behind me.

I turned to find Judy Bloomers ogling me. Her right index finger was busy twirling a lock of "secret" black hair hidden underneath her otherwise frazzled, bleached-blonde bird's nest.

"Nope. Going to a redneck cookout. Hey. Wait a minute. Are you following me? First writing class. Now the grocery store...."

Judy adjusted the girdle-tight elastic on the waistband of her sky-blue polyester slacks. "Tailing someone is next week's assignment. And for the record, I was in class before *you* got there. In fact, I believe I beat you by a solid week."

I nodded my concession. "Fair enough. Have you got your five ways to kill someone yet?"

Judy's pouty lip twitched. "Three. You?"

"Four and a half. Hey. Do you think you could kill someone with Ty-D-Bol?"

Judy smirked. "With or without the new scrubbing bubbles?"

I snorted. "What are you doing here, anyway? You don't look like you're shopping."

"Good observation," Judy said. "But wrong conclusion. I *am* shopping. Shopping for *leads*."

"Leads?"

"Sure. Every place is good for finding real estate leads. At least, that's what my broker says."

Judy picked up a can of pickled herring, realized what it was and crinkled her nose. She put it back on the shelf and shrugged.

"That's kind of why I took the class. To scope out the students. I didn't know the class would be so small."

"Huh. Any prospects?"

Judy grinned. "Clarice, the redhead, has been living alone in the same apartment since 1987. Victoria, the other lady, defers all major decisions to her husband, and he's wedged into his house like an ornery hermit crab. Old lady Langsbury's too cranky to consider. But Jeff's got potential. He's a Millennial, you know. Probably doesn't even own a car. But right about now, his parents may be reaching their critical desperation threshold and could consider buying him a cheap condo."

"Wow. You really know how to work a room."

"You missed introductions last week. It was like true confessions."

"So, are you gonna stay in class? Now that you have your leads?"

"I dunno."

"I think you should, Judy. You're a natural-born detective."

Judy smiled. "Really? Thanks."

"So, what about me?"

Judy looked me up and down, uncertainty knitted her brow. "What *about* you?"

"You have the others pegged," I said. "What are your conclusions about me?"

"Given your bulging jeans and loose-fitting top, I'd say you've been avoiding writing and pretty much eaten everything in your house that wasn't nailed down. Thus, the trip to the grocery store."

"Damn. You're good."

Judy beamed. "I try."

I blew out a breath. "That's it. I'm heading to the diet food section. I need to lose ten pounds."

I took off down the aisle with Judy on my heels.

"You're going about it all wrong," Judy called after me. "The diet thing, I mean. It's like selling real estate. You have to sell yourself the fantasy, not the reality."

I stopped in front of an aisle display laden with rows of diet food bars and canned shakes.

"What do you mean, Judy?"

"You have to sell *yourself* on an idea for it to work for you."

"I still don't get it."

"Okay. Think about it this way," Judy said, eyeballing the display. "Which idea motivates you more? Would you rather go on a diet to lose ten pounds of ugly fat, or to look like Jennifer Aniston?"

"I'll take Jennifer."

"Exactly my point."

Judy grabbed a can and a packet off the shelf and held them up about even with her shoulders.

"See what I mean?" She toggled the can in her hand. "This chocolate shake is doing it right. Drink chocolate, lose weight! What's not to like?"

"Okay."

She waggled the packet in her other hand.

"Now, look at the kale chips. Eat nasty green globs and wish you were dead."

I smirked. "I think I get it."

"Good." Judy put the can and packet back on the shelf. "Well, I better get going. I think I see a lead."

"Oh. Okay. Good luck. See you Thursday?" I called as Judy walked away.

"Pretty sure," she said, not looking back as she made a beeline for a woman with a Prada purse.

I loaded a dozen chocolate shakes in my cart and finished shopping.

At home, I unpacked my groceries, then opened my file labeled *Five Unique Ways to Kill Someone*.

Under number five, I deleted the word "Ty-D-Bol" and typed in "Kale."

Chapter Five

"Oh, dear lord of the flies," I whispered, and nudged Tom's arm. Usually annoyingly cheerful and dependable, Tom was in one of his typical good moods. He was whistling a tune as he polished the driver's side mirror of his SUV.

Unlike me, he was making good use of his time while we waited in the driveway for Laverne. She was catching a ride with us over to Winky's place.

I nudged Tom again, locked eyes with him, and bobbed my head discretely to the left a couple of times. Tom got my drift and shot a glance in that direction. His jaw went slack and his whistling hissed out like a punctured tire.

Laverne was picking her way across the lawn. In her liver-spotted hands, she held a red serving platter mounded with cookies.

"She's baked again," Tom said absently. "That explains the dead possum in the backyard."

"Ugh," I moaned. "I really don't want another bowel blowout. Especially not at Winky's place."

"I've got this," Tom said. He turned and smiled graciously at Laverne. "There you are! I'm glad you're riding over to the cookout with us. Here, let me take that for you."

"Thank you, honey!" Laverne beamed him a full set of dentures and handed over the potentially lethal plate of snickerdoodles.

Tom opened the back door of the SUV and held it for Laverne like a fancy chauffeur. "Please. Climb aboard, ma'am."

Laverne grinned. "Nice to see there's still a few gentlemen left in the world."

She scooted her scrawny butt into the backseat. Tom closed the door, then looked across the hood and shot me an evil smirk.

I tilted my head and scrunched my eyebrows. "What's up?" I whispered.

"Don't worry," Tom said. "Just get in."

I sighed, and, for once, did as I was told.

"You excited about the party?" I asked Laverne as I climbed into the front passenger seat.

"You bet! I don't get out much since J.D. moved in."

"Right." I watched Tom as he went around to the back of the SUV, opened the hatchback and closed it again.

"Here we go," he said, and climbed into the driver's seat.

My stomach gurgled like an angry bobcat. Tom laughed and turned the key in the ignition.

"This ought to be fun," he said, and backed slowly out of the drive.

"I can't wait to see Winky's place," Laverne chirped from the back seat. "I heard he's got his own swimming pool!"

"Wow!" I shook my head. "Imagine that. A few weeks ago he didn't even have his own shirt."

"Life can be unpredictable," Tom said, and turned onto Bimini Circle.

We rode in contented silence for a while as the silver 4Runner thrummed steadily along under Tom's guidance. But about a mile or so down the road, Tom suddenly turned the steering wheel sharply to the left and hit the brakes. I got a close-up view of the dashboard as the SUV first swerved, then lurched to a stop.

"Sorry about that!" Tom said, and winked at me. "Everybody okay?"

"I think so," Laverne said, patting down her strawberry-gold curls. "What happened?"

"I thought I saw a possum about to meet his maker," Tom replied, watching Laverne through the rearview mirror. "Had to swerve to miss him."

Tom locked eyes with me and grinned like a fox. "Look," he whispered, and nodded toward my side-view mirror.

I peeked just in time to see the reflection of a red plastic plate tumbling down the road behind us like a renegade hubcap.

"Poor little critter," Laverne said. "Did you miss him?"

"Yes," Tom said, and shifted into drive. "But it was a close call."

I looked back at Laverne. She was smiling brightly. I squeezed Tom's thigh and smirked.

"Yep," I said. "That was a close call, indeed."

WITH OUR DEADLY CARGO dutifully jettisoned, Tom's SUV headed north along Gulf Boulevard past rows of pastel-hued mom-and-pop hotels built during decades that seemed more innocent and less commercial than today. Tucked between the cheerful, homey motels were small shops selling beachwear and souvenirs, as well as a handful of restaurants with names like Grouper's and Barnacle Bill's, focused not so much on cuisine as on gimmicks to lure the tourists in.

It was nearly six o'clock. The sky over the Gulf of Mexico was just starting to tinge pink like a slow-boiling shrimp. Tom hooked a right at the Thunderbird Hotel and headed east. We crossed a pair of small bridges traversing the Intracoastal Waterway, leaving behind the sandy strip island and entering the mainland of Pinellas County.

As we did, everything beachy and touristy disappeared, as if the Gulf waters had been only a mirage. In place of surf-shops and beach stands, a hodge-podge of dry cleaners, banks, grocery stores and thrift shops sprouted up like toadstools. Except for the tell-tale palm trees, you could have been forgiven for thinking you were in Georgia, or D.C., or pretty much anywhere else in the good old US of A. Until you rolled down the window, that is, and got blasted by heat normally found only inside a pizza oven.

I suppose the summer heat and humidity were the only things that had kept St. Petersburg from turning into Lower New York City. That and a distinct lack of space for urban sprawl.

Pinellas County itself was comprised mostly of a bloated peninsula that stuck out of Florida's west coast and into the Gulf of Mexico like a bratty kid's swollen tongue. Bordered on three sides by water, it stretched along the coastline northward, from its southern tip, St. Petersburg, to its northern boundary, the Greek-themed town of Tarpon Springs.

The Pinellas beach towns lucky enough to stick their toes in the Gulf had enjoyed the glamour, acclaim and "progress" that tourist dollars inevitably wrought.

The opposite fate had befallen their land-locked cousins.

These turf-town communities had remained virtually ignored for decades, left to play a second fiddle so distant that it might as well have been in an orchestra on the moon. And no place played that second fiddle better than the township of Pinellas Park. An oasis of local yokels and rednecks surrounded by a desert of tourists and transplants, it was, naturally, where Winky had chosen to set up his new home-sweet-home.

Tom turned off US 19 at the Pinellas Park exit and took a left. Immediately, the view was blighted with deep-discount stores, fast-food restaurants and auto repair shops. Each proudly vied for our attention with garish lights and grammatically incorrect signs. After dodging a rusty red pick-up that nearly rammed us on its hell-bent journey to Walmart, Tom turned off 19 and onto a road sandwiched between two strip centers as tired and uninspired as a long-term life insurance salesman.

To my surprise, just one building in from US 19, the neighborhood turned residential. Its modest homes were proudly working class. Yards were un-landscaped, but tidy—not counting the occasional vehicle that hadn't moved since the turn of the millennium.

A few blocks further down the road, the yards got bigger, but the houses remained modest. We drove past a series of acre-sized plots surrounded by chain-link fences. Most were pocked with disused RVs, flower beds lined with old tires and the random mongrel dog or three.

I knew we had to be getting close when I saw the first family-pack of ATV's parked under a tin-roofed shed. That was the unquestionable signature of a well-to-do hillbilly if there ever was one.

"This is it," Tom said, and pulled into the open gate of a chain-link fence bordering a grassy, green acre.

I smiled. True to his word, Winky had gotten himself a brand-new doublewide trailer. Even in the fading light, it shone like an aluminum-clad beacon amongst his neighbors' slightly more aged residences.

Tom parked the SUV in the dirt driveway next to an equally shiny new red Camaro. Winky had bought it at Hopkins Chevrolet. I could tell because he'd modified the complimentary vanity plate. By removing the K and S, he'd turned "Hopkins" into "Hop in."

"Here we go," I said, grinning before I even climbed out of the car. I'd barely slammed the SUV door shut when the front door of Winky's trailer flew open as if it'd been kicked out by a SWAT team.

"Welcome to our humble abode," the pudgy, freckle-covered redneck hollered. "Wooo hoooo! Glad y'all made it!"

Winky looked so ready to explode with unabashed pride that I cringed involuntarily. I grinned and took him by the hand.

"Nice duds," I said, and meant it. To my utter amazement, Winky had on clean cargo shorts and a t-shirt with no stains or holes anywhere to be found. The shirt even had both sleeves still attached. I secretly worried that perhaps his money had gone to his head....

"What? This old thang?" Winky said and scratched his belly, dislodging my concerns along with the lint ball that had been inhabiting his navel. "Y'all come on in!"

"I'll get the food," Tom said as he helped Laverne climb out of the SUV. "I've been here already, so why don't you two ladies go enjoy the tour?"

"Don't mind if I do," Laverne said. "Thanks, Tom. Now keep your mitts off those cookies until you've had your dinner," she scolded playfully.

"I promise," Tom said and looked at me. "Cross my heart and hope *not* to die."

THE SMELL OF PLASTIC and formaldehyde emanating from the shiny new doublewide trailer burned my eyes, but not nearly as bad as the décor. I blinked twice to stop the stinging. Nope. The couch still didn't look any better.

"I paid extry for the stain proofin," Winky said proudly.

"You don't say," I coughed, too stunned to cobble a real sentence together. Given the sofa's hideous upholstery, a swirling pattern of orange, red and brown akin to vomit caught in a tornado, a stain didn't have a chance against it. In fact, I would have bet good money someone could have been stabbed to death on that couch and the cops wouldn't even notice.

I made a mental note to add that to my list for my writing class when I got home.

"Well, I have to say, the couch goes perfectly with the lamps," I said, trying not to stare. Perched on a side table at one end of the sofa stood a lamp made out of a stuffed raccoon. Its claw-like hands had been fashioned to hold a small, round object, the purpose of which I found myself harboring zero curiosity over. The other lamp, it pained me to say, was ET the extraterrestrial, sitting in what looked to be an empty pie tin.

"Huh. I didn't know they made shag carpet anymore," Laverne said to Winky, allowing me a moment to compose myself.

"Orange is...a bold color," I fumbled.

"Thanky," Winky said, and hitched his thumbs in his pockets. "You know, I had it special ordered. All this stuff, really."

"You're kidding," Laverne muttered. Her pug eyes looked as big as boiled eggs as she stared warily at the raccoon lighting fixture. "What were you...uh...was your *inspiration?*"

Winky grinned like a hillbilly with a jug full of corn liquor.

"Home," he said. "You see, I showed the fellers down at Fred's Furniture pictures of my mom's place back in Kentucky. I had 'em recreate it best they could. The whole place is like this. 'Cept for the kitchen. That's Winnie's domain."

"Oh," I said. "Well, I tell you what, it really *is* something."

"You ain't seen *nothin'* yet!" Winky said. "Come in here, y'all, and I'll show you my pride and joy."

Laverne and I exchanged doomed glanced, then followed Winky dutifully down a step into a sunken living room off the main trailer. The 1970s time-warp continued. On the far wall, covered with dark-brown wood paneling, an off-centered hodge-podge collection of framed sports figures hung like offerings in a thrift shop. Below them were three white, waist-high, glass-topped coolers like the ones I'd seen in convenience stores.

"Go ahead, gals," Winky offered. "They's unlocked and loaded!"

Laverne and I made our way cautiously toward the coolers and peered through their clear, sliding lids. One was full of Pabst Blue Ribbon. The other two were filled to the gills with bottles of Mountain Dew and Yoo Hoo chocolate-flavored drinks.

"Thanks, Winky," I said and slid open the beer cooler. Laverne and I each grabbed a can.

"Yeppers. This here's my man cave," Winky said, hooking his fingers in his belt loops and thrusting out his barrel chest.

"You want one?" I asked.

"Don't mind if I do." He took the beer, cracked open the tab and walked to a door beside the coolers. He opened it to reveal a pantry stuffed to the brim with beef jerky, corn nuts, pork rinds, and moon pies—the four basic redneck food groups.

"Help yoreself," he said. "And looky here."

Winky waved his right arm at a wall like a used car salesman pimping the "deal of the day."

"I had this here entertainment center built custom to hold my new sixty-five-inch, big-screen TV," Winky boasted. "And, a course, my entire NASCAR Big Gulp collection."

I'd never seen so many plastic cups in one place, much less lined up on shelves like bowling trophies.

"I got 'em all, 'ceptin' Dale Earnhardt."

"Impressive," I offered.

Winky nodded and motioned toward a half-dozen easy-chairs clad in brown corduroy.

"Each a these babies is decked out with cup-holders, massage action, and built-in TV trays," Winky gushed. "This here's my home theater. Ain't she somethin'?"

"She's something, all right," Laverne said.

"Y'all just grab a seat and relax," Winky said and picked up a TV remote. "I think *Duck Dynasty's* about to come on."

My mouth was still hanging open when Goober nudged me from behind.

"Breathtaking, wouldn't you say?" he whispered.

I turned and eyed my peanut-headed friend. "I'll give Winky this. He certainly has left me at a loss for words."

Chapter Six

"Don't tell me you're *jealous*," Goober said. His eyes danced in the moonlight beneath a pair of caterpillar eyebrows. He'd trailed behind me as I'd escaped out the back door of Winky's tin-can condo before *Duck Dynasty* came on and I was forced to watch the shenanigans of even *more* wealthy rednecks.

The wooden porch we stood on afforded a good view of the humongous back yard. A sprinkling of lightning bugs blinked flashes of reddish-yellow in the dusky sky, making me realize I hadn't seen a firefly in ages.

Across the wide expanse of lawn, Jorge and Sherryl were talking to Winnie beside a folding table laden with food. A glance to the left made me smile. Winky had outfitted his little chunk of country paradise with a tiki hut just like mine. He'd also pimped his place with a massive outdoor grille, a fire pit, and, just as Laverne had said, a swimming pool. It was an above-ground one with a fancy, redwood deck.

"No, I'm not jealous, Goober," I answered. "I'm glad for Winky. I was just desperate for a breath of fresh air. His place has that new-car smell. I don't need to be inhaling any more chemical fumes. I've got enough brain damage as it is."

"Roger that," Goober said. "I'd say from the looks of it, we all have."

I smirked at my tall, lanky friend who hid his intellect as if it were the map to the lost treasure of El Dorado. Despite his apparently solid brain and body, in all the time I'd known him, Goober had never held down a steady job.

When I'd left my glorified file-clerk post at the accounting firm of Griffith & Maas, I'd recommended him to fill the position. My friend and boss, Milly Halbert-Pantski, had hired him on a trial basis. Given his track record, I wondered which one of them was having more trials with their current arrangement.

"So, how do you like working for Milly?" I asked.

"Okay, I guess." Goober sighed and scratched the armpit of his white t-shirt. "But then again, I never have taken too well to domestication."

"What do you mean? Don't tell me you're finding it hard to fill my shoes."

Goober grinned. "You *do* have some pretty big feet. But sorry, Val. Your sensible pumps just aren't my style. I'm more of a trashy, rhinestone-studded stiletto man myself."

"Ha ha." I laughed drolly and tried to will myself not to look at Goober's feet, but I couldn't resist. The off chance that he was in hooker high heels was too good to miss. Come to find out, he wasn't wearing any shoes at all. A ping of disappointment made my gut loosen.

"What's the problem, then? Don't like the idea of a having a work wardrobe, eh?"

"No, it's more the whole, 'Be there at a certain time,' bit." Goober ran a hand across his bald pate as he spoke. "All that, 'Do this, don't do that,' stuff rubs me the wrong way."

I shrugged. "You'll get used to it."

"Did you?" Goober studied my face as he smoothed his bushy moustache with his right thumb and forefinger.

I sneered and he looked away and shrugged. "Maybe I will. Maybe I won't. Anyway, how's *your* new career going? Written any best-sellers yet?"

I blew out a breath. "Not quite. But I *did* sign up for a class on how to write mystery books for fun and profit."

"Intriguing." A bushy, angular eyebrow raised on Goober's forehead, giving me an idea of what Spock might have looked like if he were bald.

"There you all are!" Winky bellowed from the open back door. "Y'all ready to eat?"

"Let the gastronomical revelry begin," Goober said with sardonic cheer. As Winky paraded past us, Goober turned to me and whispered. "Quick. Tell me. Which one did Laverne bring?"

"No worries," I whispered. "The target has been destroyed."

"Nice work, Fremden," Goober replied. "Remind me to give you a raise."

"...AND BLESS OUR GOOD brother Old Joe," Winky prayed over the table full of food, "Who if'n he hadn't up and died and left me his bait shack, none of this would a been possible. Amen."

"Amen," everyone echoed.

"Hey. Where's the cookies I brought?" Laverne asked Tom as we lined up to receive our portion of the evening's redneck bounty.

"The Lord works in mysterious ways," Tom said. "Don't say anything, but I think Winky went and hid them, to, you know, keep them all for himself."

Laverne shot a dirty look at the back of Winky's head.

"He's got a thing for snickerdoodles," I said. "And he heard yours are the best."

Her horsey face softened into an impish, motherly smile. "Oh, that Winky. Okay. I won't mention it."

I exchanged glances with Tom, then turned and tapped Jorge on the shoulder. He was ahead of me in the buffet line. "Hey, Jorge. What did you bring?"

"Hey. Me and Sherryl brought homemade picadillo."

"Mmm! That sounds great!"

I was sure it was. Jorge was a great cook. His picadillo meant there was something on the buffet that didn't contain Karo syrup, Crisco, pork by-products, or red dye number 87. *Yes!*

"How about you?" Jorge asked.

"That tray of chocolate-drizzled strawberries, banana chunks and marshmallows," I answered.

"Good to know." Jorge took a fork and filled his plate from my tray. Soldiers in arms needed to stick together.

"What's that orange stuff that looks kind of like dried-up macaroni and cheese?" I asked Jorge.

"Sherryl told me Winnie made it. It's Cheeto squares."

"What?" I asked as I heaped a mound of picadillo into the biggest section of my fancy, Chinet-brand paper plate.

"She said it's made of melted marshmallows and Cheetos," Jorge explained as I stared at him dumbly. "You know. Like Rice Krispy squares, only you use Cheetos instead."

"Oh. I see."

Ugh. If that glop had been topped with hotdog slices, it would have had all the makings of a well-rounded redneck meal.

AFTER WAITING HALF an hour after dinner, Winky cordially invited us all to take a dip in his pool. I'm not sure what the waiting was about. There was no danger of drowning. I was only five-foot, two inches, and the water barely came up to my shoulders. Besides, if the rest of the group was in my state of gastric distress, they all had recently inflated their built-in flotation devices. I, personally, had enough gas in my bowels to keep me afloat all the way to Cuba.

Irritatingly, Jorge's stunningly beautiful girlfriend Sherryl seemed immune to both flab and flatulence.

I'd been keeping an eye on her like the jealous wife of a cheating husband. Something just wasn't right about her. I knew from careful observation that Sherryl had eaten enough food to choke a goat, yet her belly had remained suspiciously—and annoyingly—flat.

So, when we'd all stripped to our bathing suits to get into the pool, I was relieved to see Goober leave his t-shirt on. I followed his lead and left mine on, too. Next to Sherryl, I needed all the camouflage I could get. Even in a one-piece suit made of inch-thick spandex, compared to Sherryl I looked like a whale caught in a tarp. If she hadn't been so nice to me the first time I met her, I could have despised her on this point alone. But she couldn't help being gorgeous, so I decided to cut her some slack.

"Nice bathing suit," I said as I climbed down the ladder into the water beside Sherryl. Her blue-black hair and silver earrings shone in the moonlight.

"Thanks," she said. "It's so hard to find one that fits right when you're a size two." Sherryl smiled at me sweetly, with no hint of malice. I wish I could have said the same about myself. She passed me a water noodle. "Goober says you're writing a book."

"Yes. Well, uh—"

"A book!" Winky bellowed from his perch inside a donut-shaped float. "Well how 'bout that! What kind a book, Val?"

"Uh...a murder mystery," I fumbled.

"Woo hoo! A murder mystery!" Winky said. "What's it called?"

I sunk down in the water to my neck, not so much out of embarrassment as to hide my arm flab. "I don't have a title yet."

Winky chortled. "Well let me help you out there. I got an idea. How about *The Mystery of the Butt Crack*, by Eileen Dover!"

Everyone laughed, causing someone to fart. I'm not saying who.

"Very funny," I snorted.

"Oh! I got it!" Goober said as he bobbed around on a float. "*Lost in the Desert*, by Rhoda Kamel."

I smirked. "Ha ha."

"I know!" Laverne said, her hand waving in the air like an eager schoolgirl. "*Case of the Frustrated Nympho*, by Anita Mann."

The pool went silent for a moment as we all stared, open-mouthed, at the old woman in a gold thong. Then, as if someone un-clicked a "pause" button, we all came back to life. Raucous laughter filled the night air, and Winky got so tickled he upturned his float. He flailed around and came up for air looking like a half-drowned rat. Winnie had to grab him by the back of his neck to keep him from slipping back under.

"You really should learn how to swim, Winky!" she scolded.

"Why? When I got *you* to save me, sugar pea." The pair made googly eyes at each other until I felt awkward.

"Well, I think that's really impressive," Sherryl said, breaking the silence. "Val, from all the stakeouts Jorge's told me he's been on with you, I think you'd make a pretty good detective."

"Thanks, Sherryl," I said.

"As long as she sticks to a keyboard," Tom interjected. He slipped across the pool and encircled me in his arms. "Promise me, Val, from now on, you'll keep your detective work to the pages in your books. Please?"

"I promise," I said.

But under the water, my fingers were crossed. And I farted.

Again.

Chapter Seven

"You've never looked more handsome," I said to Tom as he walked into the bedroom Saturday morning.

"I bet you say that to all the guys with cappuccinos," he quipped.

I smiled coyly. "No. Only the ones with *two*."

Tom flashed his boyish grin and handed me a cup. He kissed my nose and climbed back into bed beside me. I settled into the pillows.

Ahh! This was my absolute favorite time of day. So many fresh possibilities lay ahead. But for the moment, the only ones that mattered had either a handsome, stubbly face or a frothy milk topping sprinkled with cinnamon. I took a sip of my cappuccino. It was perfection in a cup.

"Mmm. Whatever you just did, keep doing it," I said.

Tom's eyes sparkled. He wagged his blond eyebrows at me. "Are you talking about the cappuccino or the—"

"Enough!" I giggled, and elbowed him, nearly sloshing my cup.

"Never enough," Tom whispered seductively.

"Really?" I pulled away long enough to take another sip of cappuccino. Then I set my cup on the nightstand and snuggled up against Tom. "Okay, then. Prove it."

Tom's left eyebrow shot up. "Are you calling my bluff?"

"No," I teased. "I'm calling your *buff*...as, 'in the.'"

"Nice one," Tom said, and gazed at me with bedroom eyes.

"Well? What are you waiting for?" I asked.

"For you to recognize my poke-her face."

"Ugh. Tom, I think that's gotta be your *worst joke ever.*"

Tom grinned. "Well then, let me make it up to you...."

"WANT TO GO WITH ME to Fred's Furniture to find a daybed?" I asked Tom as he emerged from the bathroom with a towel wrapped around his taut waist.

"Uh...you know shopping's not my thing."

"I know," I sulked. To be honest, it wasn't mine, either. But I was eager to kill the last impediment distracting me from writing. Once I had the new daybed all set up, I'd have no more excuses.

"Suit yourself," I called after Tom as he padded to the bedroom. I opened a notebook on the desk in my home office and wrote down another unique way to die; "Paralysis by procrastination."

Not great, I thought, as I set the pen down.

I took a step toward the door and tripped over one of Tom's moving boxes stacked along the wall. Ever since that horrible escapade at Tony's Hoarder House of Horrors, aka, *the house I now live in*, anything that smacked of clutter had sent a panic-wave of claustrophobia shooting through me.

Just like now.

"Tom! Promise me you'll get rid of these boxes while I'm gone!" I yelled a little too shrilly.

"I promise!" I heard him call from the bedroom.

I walked to the kitchen, grabbed my purse and keys looked around for my sunglasses. The last time I had them I was...crap! At Winky's place. I picked up my cellphone.

"Winky?"

"Hey there, Val pal!"

"Great party last night."

"Thanky!"

"You have an awesome place," I said.

My grandmother had taught me that a proper Southern woman was always on the ready with a carefully prepared compliment for her discourse companion—even if she had to sugar-coat a turd, or paint a lie white.

"Winky, your home is like...a country retreat in the heart of the city."

"You should see my other one!"

"*Other* one? Are you saying you have *another* place?"

"Yep. It's a little getaway in the woods called Shell Hammock."

"Really? Where's that?"

"Over in Polk County. I seen it on line when I was lookin' for a place for me and Winnie to put our new doublewide. It looks real nice, Val. On a big ol' lake, too, with a fishin' dock."

"Sounds pretty. Why didn't you two just move there?"

"Well, we's business folk now, Val. Got to run the bait shop. Besides, Winnie wanted her a brand-new trailer. And a feller needs a place to run off to, now and again."

"Run off to?"

"You know, to collect his thoughts. Catch a few bream 'n' catfish. Have a few beers..."

Scratch his balls.

"...so I thought, what the heck, I'll get me *both* places."

"Huh. Good for you. So, what's it like there?"

"I don't rightly know. I ain't been there yet. But my cousin Sammy said it was real nice. He had a place there a while back. You and Tom are welcome to go up and stay at mine any time you want."

"Thanks, Winky. I just might take you up on that."

"All righty, then! But listen, I gots to go."

"Okay. Tell Winnie thanks again for the party from me."

"Will do."

I clicked off the phone and shook my head. I couldn't decide which was more astounding. Winky with a *first* home, or Winky with a *second* one.

Dang it! I forgot to ask about my sunglasses!

SUNDAY NIGHT, I FINISHED painting the last of the cut-in work along the baseboards. My office was now a cheerful, limey shade of green that matched the print on the new coverlet for the daybed I'd found at Fred's Furniture. It was scheduled to be delivered tomorrow morning.

Tom had offered to help paint, but I'd wanted to do it all on my own. I closed the paint can and looked at my tidy desk. I admired the writing schedule I'd etched out on my calendar for the week, as well as the new system of punishment and reward I'd devised to encourage my steady work progress.

Punishment was a thick, red rubber band I'd removed from a head of broccoli. I planned to wear it around my wrist and snap it if I caught myself procrastinating. Reward was a sparkling jar of colorful jelly beans. I'd get to have one for every thousand words I wrote.

I smiled, gathered up my paint brushes and drop cloth, and turned out the light.

Yes. I had everything in place to assure my writing success.

Chapter Eight

By 10:00 a.m. Monday morning, I'd been on a roll on my computer for nearly two hours. In that time, I'd won three games of *Klondike* in a row, completed *Spider Solitaire* in under two minutes, and cleared eight boards on *TriPeaks*.

And my wrist was redder than the band of rubber encircling it like a medieval torture device.

I was drawing back the band to snap it again when I thought I heard a noise. I glanced out the door toward the kitchen. I was fairly certain the pickles in the fridge were calling my name....

I snapped the rubber band around my wrist. "Ouch!" I screeched. "That really hurt!"

I clicked off the computer games. My finger hovered shakily over the Open File button. Then I realized something.

What was I thinking? There's no use getting started writing when Fred's delivery could show up any moment and blow my train of thought, right?

Are you kidding? Val, you don't have a train *of thought. You don't even have a* tricycle *of thought!*

Great. Now I'm not just talking to myself. I'm arguing with myself!

I sucked in a determined breath and planted my feet on the floor.

Your butt's not going anywhere, missy! Write something!

I wracked my brain for ideas. Where could I get inspiration for a story?

53

Wait a minute. What was the name of that place Winky talked about? Shell Hammock?

I googled it.

It was a trailer park. But it was the nicest looking trailer park I'd ever seen.

A narrow, rustic, sandy road wound through what looked to be about two acres of huge, ancient oak trees. Along the little country lane sat rows of shiny, well-kept trailers. Some were singlewides, some no bigger than an RV pull-behind. A few were doublewides. Each had quaint, carved wooden plaques hanging by their doors with slogans like, "Home Sweet Home," "Our Little Slice of Heaven," and "Welcome to Paradise."

Shots of the grounds looked equally idyllic. Wooden swings beckoned from shady spots under the trees. A sparkling lake boasted a small marina and fishing dock. A little strip of sandy beach along the lakeshore was adorned with lounge chairs and umbrellas. There was also a shuffleboard court and a pool. A sandwich board in front of the cute clubhouse sported a hand-written message that read: "Blueberry Pancake Breakfast this Sunday."

A rap at the door caught me by surprise. I peeked through the blinds. A Fred's Furniture truck was idling in my driveway. I turned off the computer, popped a jelly bean in my mouth, and headed for the door.

THE HUMID MAY AIR WAS busy turning my hair into a Brillo pad as I tooled down Central Avenue with the top down.

I hadn't gotten any writing done, but at least my daybed was set up and the nasty old bed was hauled away. My office was officially complete. And I was going to start writing as soon as I got back from lunch with Milly.

I pulled into the parking lot at Ming-Ming's sushi right next to Milly's red Beemer. As I walked up, I spied her through the plate-glass window. She was sitting at a tiny table for two. I waved and a thought struck me.

I don't think I've ever seen my friend's cute, blonde, button-nosed face look so perfectly content.

"You look like you're in a good mood," I said as I leaned down and gave her a hug.

"I am!" Milly said. "Two fantastic things just happened."

"What?"

"All of Charmine's puppies got their last shots and a clean bill of health yesterday," Milly beamed like a proud mamma. "They'll be ready to go in two weeks."

"That's great!" I pictured the six red-gold balls of mostly Pomeranian fluff and smiled.

"Have you and Tom decided on a name for yours yet?"

I pulled out a chair to sit. "No. It's so hard. It's like naming a kid!"

Milly smirked. "Tell me about it." Her face suddenly shifted gears. "Oh my lord! Look at that guy," she whispered. "There ought to be a law against dressing like that. Someone call the fashion police!"

I looked over at the man in Milly's crosshairs. He had on a hideous, pineapple-themed Hawaiian shirt, purple-and yellow plaid shorts, and Kermit-green tennis shoes.

"No way," I said, shaking my head. "That's too hideous to not be deliberate, Milly."

Milly blanched. "What are you saying?"

"I'm saying I think someone dressed him like that intentionally."

"Why?"

"So no woman would come near him."

Milly studied me for a moment.

"Just a theory, mind you," I backtracked.

Milly grinned. "Well, look at you, Miss Detective!" She took another look at the man's decently attractive face. "You know, it makes sense now. Who do you think did it? His wife?"

"Most likely. Or his girlfriend." A thought struck me. *Was JD doing the same thing to Laverne? Dressing her in frog suits to keep other men away?*

"What are you thinking now, Sherlock?" Milly stared at me, a smile gracing her pouty lips.

"Huh? Oh. Sorry. Nothing. Hey, you said you had *two* fantastic things to report. What's the second thing?"

Milly wagged her perfect eyebrows. "Goober came in and quit this morning."

My mouth fell open. "What? I'm sorry!"

"Why?"

"I recommended him and—"

Milly reached across the table and touched my hand. "Don't be sorry, Val. *I'm* not."

I cringed. "Was he *that* bad?"

Milly rolled her eyes. "Let's just say, next time I'll try my luck with a chimpanzee."

"Geez!"

"Moving on. How's the writing going?"

A scowl flew across my face. "Argh! I hate that question!"

Milly laughed. "Touch a nerve?"

"More like stomped on one. I'm telling you, Milly, I feel like I've trapped myself in my own jail cell. I've been piddling around for a week and what have I got? Exactly squat, that's what."

"Huh. Maybe you should go on that writer's retreat you told me about."

"I don't have *eighteen* dollars to waste, much less eighteen-hundred."

Milly crinkled her nose. "It's not a *waste*, Val. Think of it as an investment in your budding career as a novelist."

"I dunno," I shrugged. "I've already blown thirty-five bucks on the class."

"Not worth it?"

"I wouldn't say that. But it's got my mind all messed up."

"How?"

"I keep seeing everything as potential plot points and murder scenes."

"Really?"

"Yeah. Like right now, I'm picturing you with a chopstick jammed in your eye."

"That's twisted."

"For a novelist, that's life."

IT WAS AFTER LUNCH, and I was in downtown St. Petersburg, cruising along Fourth Street, in search of inspiration. In other words, instead of writing, I was wasting time. Finally, Southern guilt got the best of me. I sighed, gave in, and swerved over to the far right lane at the corner of First Avenue North.

As I waited for the light to turn so I could head toward home, I saw Goober come out of the post office on the corner.

He didn't notice me.

I was about to honk when I saw him stop and drop something into the trash bin outside. Suddenly, the hair on my arms pricked up. A predatory thrill shot through me. I was a cat hunting a mouse. No...I was Valliant Stranger, on the trail of the elusive Goober Man!

Okay, maybe it was a little nutso. But it beat going home to a blank computer screen.

I hooked a sharp right, barreled across three lanes and glided into a fifteen-minute parking slot. I jumped out of Maggie and sprinted up to the trash can. I shoved in a fist and came up with a handful of envelopes. I stuffed them into my purse and looked up.

Goober still hadn't spotted me.

He ducked into an alley. I hightailed it to the corner he'd disappeared behind and peeked around it like I'd seen cops do in the movies.

Nothing.

I couldn't have been more than ten seconds behind him, but he was gone. I glanced back toward my car. A meter maid with a golf cart and a god complex was giving me the evil eye. The spot Maggie was parked in was marked Post Office Customers Only.

"Wait! I'm coming!" I yelled at the parking patrol lady as I dashed back to my car.

I showed her the handful of envelopes. "See? I was at the post office."

Her sneer turned to a doubtful glare.

"I'm leaving, see?" I offered, and climbed into my car. I turned the ignition and my phone started ringing. I waved goodbye to Brunhilda the meter monster and pulled out onto First Avenue, then clicked on the phone.

"Hello?"

"Hey, Val. Did you leave your sunglasses at our place?"

"Oh. Hi Winky. Yeah, I think I did."

"I got 'em here at the donut shop if you want 'em."

"Great. I'm on my way."

Chapter Nine

I pulled into the parking lot at Caddy's and smugly flashed the attendant my badge.

"What's that?" a voice asked from beneath an orange sun visor and a bulbous nose pasted white with zinc oxide.

"I park for free," I said.

"Let me see that."

The young guy grabbed the wallet from my hand. "That's nothing but a toy sheriff's badge."

I swiped the wallet back. "Check with your boss. I'm a donut-shop VIP. It's in the contract."

He took a step back to let me pass. "Okay, lady. If you're that desperate to save five bucks, go ahead."

A snooty smirk crept across my lips. I slapped my wallet closed, rumbled Maggie's dual glasspacks for good measure, and idled into a parking spot in the crushed-shell lot next to Winky's red Camaro. The salty aroma of the Gulf of Mexico filled my nostrils, and between wisps of waving sea oats, the sun played on the gentle waves, making the water glisten like acres of diamonds.

I shook my head softly, lost in admiration for my little spot of heaven on earth. Sugar-white sand. Turquoise water. Near permanent sunshine. Yeah, Sunset Beach had to be one of the most gorgeous places on the planet.

A seagull cried out in the sky above. I looked up toward the cloud-less blue sky. A white squirt of bird poop splattered my windshield, putting an exclamation point on the end of my daydream.

"Figures."

I cut the ignition and checked my face in the rearview mirror. Not as bad as I'd expected. I wiped a smudge of mascara from beneath my left eye and climbed out of Maggie's red bucket seat. I smoothed the wrinkles creasing the lap of my yellow gingham sundress and flounced by the man in the orange visor, my nose in the air.

"I know the proprietors," I said and nodded toward Winnie and Winky's Bait & Donut Shop.

My impudent eyes to the sky, I didn't see the kid's plastic shovel sticking out of the sand. My sandal caught the handle dead center like a stirrup. My foot hopelessly entangled, I fumbled around like a lame horse until I tripped, lost my balance, and stepped down hard on the cheap shovel. It snapped in half and launched me forward, arms out like Frankenstein.

I landed in the sand on my hands and knees.

Geez! At least I didn't eat a dirt sandwich.

As I contemplated my good luck, it ran out. A gust of wind blew my dress up to my waist. I cringed crimson. I hadn't done laundry in a while and was down to my "Sunday Survival Panties."

In other words, my bloomers were as holy as the head nun at a moth sanctuary.

Between the intermittent thumping sounds in my eardrums, I caught pulses of hysterical laughter emanating from the direction of the lot attendant. I scrambled to my feet, dusted myself off, and didn't look back.

"HEY, VAL PAL!" I HEARD Winky bellow as I walked up to the little shack formerly known as Old Joe's Bait and Tackle.

I grinned.

Leave it to Winky to get half a million bucks for a place that looks as if it were cobbled together from washed-up debris. One man's trash was Winky's treasure.

"Good lord a mighty, woman!" Winky said, staring at my face. "Ain't you heard of sunscreen?"

I shrugged. I knew the red face I sported was only temporary. "It'll pass," I said. "How's biz?"

"Fair to middlin'." He shrugged, then laughed. "All right. Purty darn good, to be honest. In fact, Winnie's done had to go to Davie's to pick up more donuts. We're fresh out."

I frowned. "Dang. I was hoping to score one of her famous peanut-butter bombs."

Winky grinned. "I knowed you was comin' Val." He reached underneath the counter. "Here's your sunglasses, and a bomb. Saved you the last one."

"You're the best," I said to both him and the donut. My mouth was already salivating.

Winky watched proudly as I sunk my teeth into the donut and enjoyed the awesome combination of peanut butter, vanilla custard and bacon. I stopped mid-chew.

"What's up with your teeth?" I mumbled.

Winky grinned and puffed out his barrel chest. "Noticed, eh? I done got me a partial."

He reached a freckled hand into his mouth and pulled out a pink-plastic and metal doohickey with a fake molar on either end. He held it up to the sunlight for me to examine as if it were the Crown Jewels of Redneckingham.

My mouthful of donut lost its flavor. "That's nice," I muttered. "You can put it back, now."

Winky popped his dentures back in his mouth and smiled. "They look all natural-like, don't ya think?"

"Sure do." I grabbed my sunglasses. "Thanks for the donut."

"Any time, Val pal."

"And thanks for bringing my sunglasses over here to the beach. That was really sweet of you."

"T'wern't nothin'."

I turned to leave, then a thought spun me back around. "Oh. Winky, I looked up your place online. Shell Hammock? It looks really nice."

"Don't it, though?" Winky scratched his belly proudly. "Oh! That reminds, me. This here's for you." He reached under the counter again and pulled out a key.

"What's this?"

"Why, it's the key to my place at Shell Hammock, a'course. I made a set fer ever'body. You and Tom is welcome to go for a visit any old time you feel like it."

I stared at the key, stunned at Winky's generosity. "Geez. Thanks." He dropped the key into my open hand. "By the way, tell Winnie I'm sorry I missed her."

"Will do."

I glanced around at the shack again, a tad more impressed. Winky fit this ramshackle old place like a hotdog fit a bun. Anyone else would have dozed the thing. But he was the perfect proprietor for it. In fact, he looked born to play that exact role.

"I just wanted to say, Winky, you've got a really cool place here. I'm happy for you."

Winky's freckled face went slack. "Shucks, Val. Compared to J.D.'s place, this ain't nothin' but a hole in the wall."

My lips twisted sideways. "J.D.'s place? Where is it, anyway?"

"Right yonder." Winky pointed a finger at some sand dunes. Beyond them sat a boxy, un-beachy, totally out-of-place McMansion the color of pumpkin puke.

"*That's* J.D.'s place?" I said, aghast. "How did I *not* know that?"

"J.D.'s a modest little feller," Winky said. "He don't go 'round braggin'."

I studied Winky and smiled. Besides some badly needed clothing, shelter and teeth, his new-found fortune hadn't changed him one bit. Thank goodness for that.

Winky swung a swatter and ended the short life of a fly crawling across the counter. "You know, Val, we business-man types don't go in fer garish displays a wealth."

"Of course not," I said. "We wouldn't want that."

EVEN AT FIFTEEN MILES an hour, the drive home was passing too quickly. I turned up the radio volume to 'deafen' and cruised down Gulf Boulevard slow enough to make the guy's face behind me turn as red as a baboon's behind. I eased off the gas and watched a sunburned tourist hobble down the molten sidewalk in ill-fitting, cheap flip-flops.

Even as paradise loomed all around me, my gut clenched with doom at what awaited me at home.

A blank computer screen.

WHEN I FINALLY PULLED up to my house, Laverne was in her front yard, talking to a bubbly washtub full of garden gnomes. I shook my head. That old woman really had a thing for short, German men. I parked and walked over under the pretenses of investigating for potential story inspiration. I tried to convince myself I wasn't stalling, but by now, even *I* was no longer buying my own bull. *Anything* seemed more compelling than writing. If Laverne had been out there clipping her toenails, I'd have still gone over.

"What are you doing?" I asked.

"These little guys needed a bath," Laverne said. She wiped sweat from her brow with a kerchief. "I love my little nomads."

"Gnomes."

"Sure. They all have names. This one's Jed." Laverne held up a fat little figure with a red stocking cap and a shovel over one shoulder.

"That's not what I meant."

"Huh?" Laverne cocked her horsey head like a curious puppy. "How's the writing—"

"Don't ask," I blurted.

Laverne shrunk back a bit.

"Sorry. It's going slower than I'd hoped."

"Oh. Sorry to hear that." Laverne scrubbed Jed's face with a brush. "Maybe you need to clean the dust out of your eyes." Laverne held up Jed for my inspection. His expression looked surprisingly crazed.

I recoiled slightly. "What do you mean?"

"Get yourself a fresh perspective, honey. Hey, why don't you go on that writer's retreat you've been talking about?"

"I'm not made of money *like J.D.*," I grumbled. "I just saw his place on the beach."

Laverne studied me with her bulgy pug eyes. Her left eyebrow angled upward. "Ugly as homemade sin, am I right?"

My own eyebrows crept up slightly. "Uh...yeah."

Laverne grinned and dunked Jed underwater and held him there like a wanton serial killer. "Our places are so much nicer, don't you think?"

I looked at her house, then mine. The knot in my stomach eased. "You're right, Laverne. Our places have character. You know, now that I'm thinking about it, even Winky's trailer has more soul than J.D.'s slapped-together box on the beach."

Laverne exposed her full set of dentures to the midday sun. "There you go.'" She pulled Jed from the water. I sucked in a sympathetic breath.

"Laverne, did you know Winky has another place? A little trailer-cabin thing in the woods. He just gave me the key and said I could go any time."

"Well, there you have it!" Laverne said, and set Jed in the grass to dry. "What are you waiting for?"

"Huh?"

"There's your *writer's retreat*, Val."

My jaw went slack. "Oh my word. You're *right*, Laverne. Thanks for the idea."

"My pleasure, honey." Laverne fished around in the tub, grabbed a gnome pushing a wheelbarrow, and began to briskly scrub his butt.

I STARED AT MY COMPUTER screen. My wrist was red and my jelly-bean jar was half empty. Apparently, inspiration only came when it darn well felt like it.

"Screw it," I muttered and reached for my phone.

I called Winky and booked his place at Shell Hammock. Then I started packing my bags. I was almost done when Tom came through the front door.

"Val? You home?" he called out.

I padded down the hall to meet him. "I'm here. But not for long."

Tom kissed me before the second half of my greeting registered. He looked at me sideways. "Not long? What are you talking about?"

I blew out a breath. "I'm frustrated, Tom. For some reason, I'm just not able to write at home. There are too many... *distractions*."

"You mean like *me*?"

My mouth twisted to one side. "I *wish* I could blame it on you. But you're not even home while I should be writing."

Tom's brow furrowed. "Then what is it?"

I thought about telling Tom about the evil pickles in the fridge. Or the jelly beans that kept jumping into my mouth. But I really saw no point in giving him any more reasons to question my sanity.

"I need a change of scenery. For inspiration."

"You mean that writer's retreat thing?"

"No. Something better. Come here. I'll show you."

I led Tom into my office and googled Shell Hammock. "Winky has a place here. He said we can go anytime."

"Wow. This place looks great," Tom said as I flipped through the pictures. I could tell he was impressed, especially when he saw the sign for the blueberry pancake breakfast. "But how will it be any different from being *here*?"

"I dunno," I whined. "Maybe it'll make me feel like a *real* writer. And if I'm going to take a writer's retreat, I need to do it *now*."

"Why?"

"I had lunch with Milly today. She said our puppy will be ready to come home in two weeks. So if I'm gonna do this, *now's* the time."

"What about your writing class?" Tom asked.

"I can get the notes from Judy." I sounded like a kid whining for a new bicycle. "I've got this week's assignment done. Actually, I've got *six* unusual ways to kill someone. And I peeked ahead at the next assignment. It's to tail someone. And I'm already working on that, too, sort of...."

Tom's left eyebrow arched. "Really? You've been tailing someone?"

I smirked. "It's not you."

"Oh. Too bad." Tom pulled me to him. "How about *I* tail *you*?"

I shook my head. "You really *do* need to work on your jokes."

"Who's joking?" Tom whispered, and nibbled my neck. "Tell me. Does this 'tailing' involve undercover work?"

A rush of desire swept through me. I wrapped my arms around Tom and whispered, "I certainly hope so."

Chapter Ten

As I watched Tom's SUV disappear down the drive, my body actually quivered with excitement. Soon, I'd be heading out on my very first writer's retreat! I wasn't merely some middle-aged woman escaping to a trailer park in the woods. I was Valiant Stranger—private detective, budding novelist, and *undercover spy.*

Oh, yeah!

And I was on special assignment to infiltrate a gang of unsuspecting, lake-loving country folks...

Bring it on!

I crammed a pair of binoculars in my duffle bag along with my laptop. My body quivered again.

Wow! I have a whole week ahead of me. Seven days to hone my detective skills, do as I darn well please, and, hopefully, peck out a short story worth sharing with old lady Langsbury's writing class next week.

I drained my cappuccino cup and headed for the shower.

After a leisurely breakfast of two blueberry Pop-Tarts and a quick peek on the internet at the latest spy gadgets, I slung my suitcase and duffle bag into Maggie's trunk and slammed it shut. All I had left to do was lock the front door and leave.

I grabbed my purse off the driver's seat and rifled through it for my keys. In the process, I pulled out a lipstick, hand lotion and a pack of corn nuts I'd lifted from Winky's the other night.

No keys.

Geez! I just had them!

I yanked out a bunch of papers clogging up my purse. They were the envelopes I'd fished out of the trash in front of the post office yesterday.

Oh yeah...

"Making your getaway, I see!" Laverne's voice rang out.

I jerked my head to the left. The once-glamorous Vegas line dancer was making a beeline for me across the lawn, clutching a plastic container in her hand.

"I brought you some snacks for your trip!" she beamed. "The last of the snickerdoodles!"

"Oh. Wow. You shouldn't have," I said. I forced a smile and crammed the envelopes back in my purse. "Thanks, Laverne. But I've really got to get going if I want to miss the rush hour traffic."

Laverne handed me the container of cookies. "So, what are you waiting for?"

A glint of something shiny made me look down. Laverne was wearing gold high heels.

Really? On a random Tuesday morning? For walking across a lawn?

"Uh...I can't find my keys."

Laverne cocked her horsey head and pointed a red lacquered fingernail toward Maggie's rear end. "They're hanging in the trunk lock, honey."

Heat thrummed my cheeks. "Oh. Thanks."

I hung my head, did "the walk of shame" to the trunk and yanked the keys from the lock.

"Have a good trip," Laverne offered as I slid my butt into the seat.

"Thanks," I muttered, and forced a smile.

As I pulled out and waved goodbye to Laverne, I felt the rest of my confidence fall away like a dead bug on the windshield. It tumbled into the gutter along the side of the road.

Geez. What kind of detective am I? Already done in by my own ineptitude...

I glanced at the plastic container of cookies in the passenger seat.

...and I can't even outrun an old lady in stilettos armed with malicious baked goods.

I ADJUSTED THE REARVIEW mirror and tried again to smile. I was making good time crossing the Howard Frankland Bridge. At least I had *that* going for me.

Interstate 275 was the main artery connecting St. Petersburg to Tampa, and was notorious for major traffic snarls. But by leaving at 10:00 a.m., I'd timed it just right. Morning rush-hour was winding down and the lunch rush had yet to begin.

The wind had whipped up whitecaps on the open expanse of Tampa Bay. But the breeze wasn't refreshing. Not even at seventy miles an hour with the top down. June was nipping at our heels. And with it came the long, steamy, dog-days of summer. The air, as hot and wet and unappealing as a hassling hound's breath, was here to stay for a good long while.

I sighed and resigned myself to it. For the next five months, I'd have to grin and bear the claustrophobic feeling of sunscreen slathered all over my skin, and the tickling annoyance of sweat perpetually trickling down my back.

Fabulous.

As I crossed the high point in the middle of the Howard Frankland Bridge, I pulled off my sunhat and let my hair blow wild and free. The wind seemed to loosen some of my doubts as well, and I allowed myself to smile.

THE GREY, SPIKEY BUILDINGS of downtown Tampa faded in the hot haze as I pulled onto I-4 and headed east. If I stayed on I-4 long enough, I'd end up at Disney World.

When I was a kid, I remembered the land between Tampa and Orlando had been blanketed with mile after mile of citrus groves. At blossom time, their sweet, honey-like fragrance would waft through the air for miles. But as I buzzed by the same stretch of land today, the orange trees were nowhere to be found. They'd been replaced by truck stops, RV dealerships and other assorted industrial blights.

Well, those and, of course, Dinosaur World.

I waved at the strangely orange Tyrannosaurus Rex peeking out over the pine trees on the left of the interstate. A few miles later, I steered Maggie off I-4 toward Plant City. Known at the Winter Strawberry Capital of the World, it wasn't surprising that the town held an annual strawberry festival around the beginning of March. Strawberry season was long gone for the year, but that was okay by me. That meant fewer tourists.

Besides, I knew a place where I could still get a strawberry shake. Parksdale Farmer's Market.

I took a small detour down Route 92 and blew my lunch calories on one of the most delectable treats imaginable (besides Minneola tangelos). When it was my turn up to bat at the counter, I thought about ordering a strawberry shortcake, too, but changed my mind. As I glanced around at the market stalls crammed with strawberry jams and jellies, I realized nearly everybody milling about the place was as thick and round and reddish-pink as the contents of the plastic cup I was rapidly sucking empty through a straw.

I needed to leave before I succumbed to the dark side....

THE COOLNESS OF THE strawberry shake felt good sandwiched between my thighs. I picked it up, sucked on the straw, and took a right on SR 39. The view immediately switched to a pastoral palette. Acre upon acre of dry, dun-colored grass was punctuated only by thirsty-looking cows kneeling in the shade of huge, centuries-old oaks with bark as rough as an alligator's hide.

At the junction to SR 60, I hooked a left and headed toward Bartow.

The seat of Polk County, Bartow was home to a handful of car dealerships and a whole mess of ugly, compliments of wanton phosphate strip-mining. As I passed yet another rusty silo, I wondered if maybe the city founders should change the phrase county "seat" to "butt-crack."

I blew through Bartow with the top still down on Maggie, and stayed on SR 60 all the way to my journey's end, Lake Wales.

The small town of Lake Wales was home to around fifteen-thousand average souls and two unique roadside attractions. One was Spook Hill, a gravity hill that created the optical illusion that your car was rolling uphill.

The other was Bok Tower Gardens. Built in the 1920s, the two-hundred-and-five-foot "singing" tower was an impressive landmark that stuck out above the trees like an old lion's tooth.

Bok Tower "sang" thanks to something called carillon bells. I'd never seen them, but I'd heard them on many occasion. They produced a throaty, flute-like sound that formed hauntingly beautiful melodies for the folks strolling around the garden's two-hundred and fifty acres. Personally, my favorite time to visit was in March, when the azaleas were in bloom.

I passed by the sign for Bok Tower Gardens and stopped for gas. A skinny man in a light-blue shirt walked up and nodded. An embroidered patch on his pocket spelled out Billy Bob.

Of course it did.

"Fill her up," I said.

"Ungh." Billy Bob grunted in a way that seemed to require the involvement of his entire torso. He looked me up and down as I climbed out of Maggie, and grunted again.

Uncertain if Billy Bob had recently escaped from a zoo or insane asylum, I scurried in to use the restroom and pay my tab. The guy at the register looked just like Billy Bob. But my eagle-sharp detective eye noticed the patch on *his* pocket read, "Jim Bob."

"Let me guess," I said. "Billy Bob's your brother."

"Ungh," Jim Bob grunted and eyed me with appreciation. "Good lookin' *and* smart."

I paid with cash and decided to skip the washroom.

As I drove away, I clicked my cellphone for a map of the vicinity. According to TripAdvisor, there were thirty-four things to "do" in Lake Wales. But from what I'd seen so far, I wasn't convinced there were thirty-four "do"-able men in all of Polk County combined.

I CHECKED THE ADDRESS on my cellphone again and shook my head. This couldn't be right.

I'd driven through Lake Wales and past miles of cow pastures and palmetto scrubland. The only signs of civilization I'd seen since the Walmart plaza had been a pair of abandoned phosphate silos and a couple of old wooden shacks with caved-in tin roofs that looked as if they'd been hit by meteors at least a decade ago.

The sun was fading to the west, spewing beams of orange and red into the thin, blue horizon.

Not good.

A shiver ran down my spine, despite the heat. Had I somehow accidently driven onto the set of *Road Warriors?*

I was about to turn around when I spied the only sign of human habitation I'd seen for miles. It was an old man selling boiled peanuts by the side of the road.

I pulled over and approached the leather-skinned old man. He was sitting in a cheap, plastic chair and appeared to be harboring a fugitive watermelon inside the waistband of his dirty overalls.

"Excuse me, sir, would you happen to know where Shell Hammock is?"

"Yep," he said, and swirled a huge, slotted spoon around in a cauldron of tea-colored water.

"Great," I said. "Could you tell me where it is?"

The man adjusted his ball cap and lifted the spoon out of the water. He plucked a couple of boiled peanuts from the heap mounded up in the spoon.

"You done found it, young lady," he said, and handed me the peanuts. My Southern upbringing forced me to take them out of politeness. They felt warm and moist and round in my hand, like a pair of fresh cat turds.

"I don't understand," I said, and cursed myself for spending an hour sorting through the Red Box videos when I'd stopped to get groceries in Lake Wales. I'd wasted precious time. Now the sky was pinkish purple and beginning to close in around me. Nightfall was coming.

If I didn't find this place soon, I'd be out of fingernails to chew off.

The old man dumped the rest of the peanuts back in the cauldron and pointed the empty spoon toward the entrance to a dirt road about thirty feet away. It looked more like a cave than a road, thanks to the canopy of scrub oaks overhanging it as if their aim in life was to swallow it whole.

"Sign's right there."

I squinted at the dark opening in the scrub. About fifteen feet above the dirt, tucked amongst the tree limbs, was an old wooden sign that spanned the width of the road like a beat-up banner. The sign read, "hell ammo."

"That says hell ammo," I said.

The old man laughed, revealing his lack of a proper dental plan.

"I forget sometimes," he said. "Yeah, lost a few letters awhile back. Now, I guess, we're the Hell'ammo."

He grinned, but I guess my expression made him realize I needed a little more convincing.

"*You* know," he said, and aimed his spoon at me like a rifle. "Like 'The Alamo.' Minus the guns."

As if on cue, a gunshot blast rang out. I flinched and bit my lip to keep from screaming as the sound echoed across the road and disappeared into the thicket of palmettoes and scrub oaks.

The old man shrugged. "Okay, *with* the guns."

My spine arched involuntarily. The whole scenario felt so wrong on so many levels I didn't know where to begin. But Valiant Stranger whispered in my ear.

If you're going to be a professional writer, Val, you can't go running home like a crybaby at every little potentially lethal discharge of a deadly firearm.

I took a deep breath, set my jaw and stepped forward. I reached out my hand.

"Hi. I'm Val. What's your name?"

I got another glimpse of the guy's woefully inadequate dental care. "Stumpy," he said. "Pleased to meet you."

Stumpy? Great. Nothing good ever came from a nickname that implied missing body parts.

He stuck out a handful of short, blunt fingers.

"Oh! On account of your fingers?" I blurted, relieved that all his digits were intact, even though they were rather...*abbreviated.*

"Huh?"

Stumpy looked at his calloused hand as if he'd never seen it before.

"Naw. Used to make statues out a cypress stumps. Sold 'em by the side of the road 'til I got too old for it. That's when I switched to peanuts."

"I see," I said, not really wanting to. "Well, do you know a fellow named Junior Whitehead? I'm supposed to let him know when I've arrived."

"Yeah. I know him purty good."

I waited a beat.

"So, can you tell me where I might find him?"

"You're lookin' at him, darlin'."

My gut fell four inches. "Oh. Well, uh...you see, my friend Winky owns number thirteen and—"

"I know all about it, hon," Stumpy said. "Just go straight on in. Take your first left, then a right at the clubhouse, then right on Possum Place. Then another right on Lonesome Pine. You'll see it. Last trailer on the left."

"Uh...thanks, mister....uh, Stumpy." I walked back to Maggie, turned the ignition, and drove slowly past Stumpy and his cauldron of drowned legumes.

Stumpy leered with bloodshot eyes as I passed by.

"Nice car you got there," he said.

I thought I heard a banjo playing. I gambled a glance in the rearview mirror. Nope. Stumpy was merely waving slowly at me with his stunted hand.

No. That wasn't creepy at all....

The dirt road was so dark I had to switch on my headlights. I followed Stumpy's directions to the letter. They led me through the entire trailer park on a windy loop that ended back where I'd begun. I looked around. Number thirteen was the first trailer on the left as you came in off the main road.

Stumpy'd just sent me on my first Polk County wild goose chase.

I scowled and pulled Maggie up beside the little trailer. As I reached to open the car door, a familiar face loomed at me in the twilight.

"Have a nice trip?" Stumpy asked.

"Nice one," I managed to squeak as my heart thumped in my throat.

Stumpy grinned. "Aw. Don't take it personal. 'Round here, a feller's got to provide his own entertainment. I was just funnin' ya."

Stumpy reached toward me. I flinched. In his hand was a moist paper bag.

"Here, have a sack of peanuts on me."

"Thanks." I took the paper bag. My face flushed with heat.

"Listen here," Stumpy said, leaning in a tad too close for comfort. "We're havin' us a big fish fry tomorrow tonight. Come 'round and meet the other folks."

"Okay, thanks. But right now, I better get these groceries inside before it gets too dark."

"Yep. Don't want to be out after dark around here," he said, and ambled off down the road.

I took a look at my new home for the week. Number thirteen wasn't a bona fide trailer. It was a pull-behind RV propped up on flat tires and cinder blocks. What had I done?

You can do this, Valliant Stranger.

I steeled myself, climbed out of the car and unlocked Maggie's trunk. I threaded the grocery sack handles up my forearms and set my suitcase on the ground.

Something rustled in the dark bushes nearby.

The hair on the top of my head stood up like a sinner at a church revival.

Adrenaline shot through my veins. The rush sent me scurrying like a wild-woman for the RV. I fumbled the door open with the key Winky had given me and threw the groceries inside. Against my own will, I made a mad dash back for my suitcase and duffle bag.

I jerked them both out of the trunk and nearly tripped over my suitcase as I slammed Maggie's trunk. I grabbed it and my duffle and skedaddled into the RV like a hobo catching the last freight train out of Dodge.

Once inside, I jerked the deadbolt in place with trembling hands and wondered out loud.

"Geez, Louise, Val. What have you gotten yourself into this time?"

Chapter Eleven

I was swimming at Sunset Beach with a school of shiny, silver fishes. We were giggling as we waggled our tails on the way to a party. I was wearing a tiara, because, of course, I was a mermaid princess....

All of a sudden, a strange network of strings surrounded us. My scaly friends and I huddled into a ball of confusion. I felt a tug. Then another. Upward we went, inch by inch, as the net drug us to the surface. I could see the sun. Then I realized I couldn't breathe!

We tumbled together into a vat...and spiraled down a dark, grey tube like water down a drain. At the end of the tube, I saw my new home. It was a sardine can. I squeezed myself inside it and lay there like cordwood alongside my companions. A squirting sound made me look up. A big glob of yellow grease splattered over us like a transparent, oily blanket.

Wait a minute. There was definitely something fishy going on....

I WOKE UP WITH A START, swimming in sweat. It was pitch black. Angry growls emanated from under the bedcovers. Either I was about to get eaten alive, or I was about to starve to death.

I shot out of bed. My shoulder whacked against a hard surface. Like a ricocheting bullet, I bounced off the wall, stubbed my toe on some unknown object, and knocked my head on the corner of something with a big corner.

What the heck was going on here?

I fumbled for the light switch. As the dim, yellow bulb blinked on, I was reminded that I wasn't in St. Pete anymore. I was in a tin-can condo the size of an ice-cream truck. But it didn't smell like Ben & Jerry's. Not unless they'd released a new flavor called Malted Moth Balls.

"Ugh!" I forced opened a tiny window in the bedroom, then hobbled along the three-foot-long hallway to the kitchen galley. I yanked opened the tiny fridge and cursed myself. Last night, I'd filled it with the salad greens, carrot sticks and diet salad dressing I'd bought in Lake Wales. I tried the cupboard, hoping against hope for some kind of junk-food miracle. Nope. Just the kale crisps and seaweed rollups I'd put in there.

What the heck had I been thinking?

After last night's "Something's in the bushes!" scare, I'd been too nervous to eat dinner. I'd cranked on the window air conditioner, fixed myself a gin and tonic and passed out on the short-sheeted bed. Sometime during the night, the A/C must have frozen up and crapped out. It was 3:09 a.m. and I was trapped in a metal box, as sweaty as a pig and as hungry as a bear.

I was a pigbear!

And all I had to cool and feed myself was a cardboard church fan and some roots and leaves.

Pigbear was not happy.

I made myself a Tanqueray and tonic. As I put the bottle back in the fridge, I noticed a soggy paper bag slumped over on the tiny dinette table like a lump of beige clay. I reached inside the bag and pulled out a boiled peanut. I popped the salty shell into my mouth, worked it open with my tongue, and bit down on the three soft, perfectly cooked pearls inside.

They were the best boiled peanuts I'd ever eaten.

I WAS SITTING IN THE dinette booth finishing off the last peanut in the sack when I heard another growl. But this time, my stomach had nothing to do with it. The grumbling had come from outside. And it sounded *very* nearby.

I switched off the kitchen light and scooted a few inches along the booth until I could press my face to the window pane. I couldn't see a dad-blame thing.

Another high-pitched, cat-like snarl pierced the night. The noise was coming from somewhere near the front end of the RV. A second later, it was followed by a tinny clunking sound. The growl sounded again, accompanied by another, deeper growl. A third whiny screech joined in.

It sounded as if a crowd of drunken chipmunks were having a rave, and then things turned ugly. I'd never heard anything like it. Unless I counted that time Winky and Jorge trapped a stray cat in a Croker sack full of empty tin cans.

I peered through the mini blinds and squinted hard. My skin turned to gooseflesh. Something as big as a human ran by in the darkness. I let go of the blinds as if they'd just stung me.

Mother of Pearl! Was there really such thing as Bigfoot?

Stumpy had warned me not to go out after dark.

And here I am...all alone! I need protection!

I scrambled around the tiny RV searching for a club. There wasn't even so much as a flyswatter. I grabbed the only thing I could find and hot-footed it back to the bedroom. I locked the door and leapt into the bed, but not before managing to stub my toe yet again on the dad-burn bedframe.

"Yow!"

I screeched in pain, then clapped a hand over my big mouth in case Sasquatch was listening. I sat up in bed and pulled my in knees in toward my chest. For the next hour, I remained there, balled up and still as a statue, breathing into the blackness, my itchy finger poised on the trigger of a spray-bottle of Ty-D-Bol.

WHEN I WOKE UP AGAIN, the sun was shining through the slits in the bedroom blinds. I sat up and looked around, pleasantly surprised to discover that I was still alive.

A tap on the door made me blink myself into focus.

Geez! I haven't even had a cup of coffee yet!

I padded to the door and opened it a tiny crack. Whoever it was didn't need to know I was wearing Tom's t-shirt as pajamas.

"Boy howdy," Stumpy said through the crack.

He was in his same dirty overalls, and still smuggling that prize-winning watermelon. But his t-shirt looked clean.

"Stinks in there," he said, and crinkled is bulbous red nose.

"It wasn't me," I lied. As tasty as they'd been, Stumpy's boiled peanuts had, nevertheless, taken their toll on my colon.

"Shut up." Stumpy replied.

How rude!

"What?" I scowled.

"Trailer's been shut up a while. Nothin' a little airin' out won't solve."

"Oh," I said. "Right."

"Came by to see how you was gettin' on. And remind you 'bout the fish fry tonight."

I opened the door a hair wider. "Okay. Thanks. What can I bring?"

"Oh, no. You're our guest tonight, young lady. You don't got to bring nothin'."

"That's really nice of you, Stumpy. Thanks. And, by the way, your boiled peanuts are really good. The best I've had, actually."

Stumpy beamed with the kind of unselfconscious pride I've only ever witnessed in the true South.

"That's what I like to hear."

"I'm curious," I said. "What's there to do around here?"

"Well, purty much anything you put your mind to."

Stumpy grinned, reminding me to make an appointment with my dentist.

"'Cept mindin' your own business, that is." He laughed. "Folks 'round here is plum allergic to that."

"Thanks for the warning. But I think they'll find me a pretty boring subject."

"I guess we'll see about that."

AFTER DOWNING A CUP of coffee and cleaning the entire kitchen and bathroom with Ty-D-Bol, bleach, and an old toothbrush I found under the sink, I got dressed and went out to explore the Hell'ammo.

It had been too dark to see squat when I'd arrived last night. But the morning light revealed the true natural beauty—and truly unnatural horror—of the place.

Tucked amongst the beautiful old live oaks and saw-leaf palmettos was what could only be described as the decaying remnants of tsunami debris.

The wave must have washed over Lake Rosalie perhaps twenty years ago. Left behind in its wake was a hodge-podge of off-kilter, rusty old trailers and abandoned household goods gone bad. As I glanced around, I got the feeling even a junkyard would turn its nose up at most of the crap gracing the property.

From what I could tell, none of the trailers or RVs had been moved in decades. How could they have been? Their tires were either flat, disintegrated, or completely AWOL.

Most of the trailers were covered in cheap, falling-down plastic siding, tacked up ages ago to make them appear more like cabins. Others, like mine, didn't bother to hide the fact they were pull-behind RVs. Either way, all were covered in a thin film of green algae, as if the forest itself was trying to slowly digest them, bit by bit.

Spanish moss hung from the trees like old hag's hair, and piled up on the rooftops like mounds of bad curly perms waiting to be donated to a senior center. The narrow spaces between the run-down abodes were clogged like arteriosclerotic veins. Not with garbage, per se, but with piles of broken furniture and rusted car parts, accented by the occasional abandoned major or minor household appliance.

I wondered what an alien from another planet would make of all this. I shook my head.

No wonder Bigfoot ran away.

I glanced over at Maggie and reminded myself that I could leave at any time. The thought made me suck in a deep, comforting breath. I noticed her rearview mirror was askew, and walked over to investigate.

Crap! Someone had been pilfering around inside Maggie!

In my haste not to become Sasquatch's bride last night, I'd left her top down. Whoever'd fiddled with her mirror had left the seats and floorboards smeared with muddy prints. I opened the passenger door. The gnawed lid of a plastic container fell out onto the ground.

Uh oh....

A noise behind me made me whip around. A raccoon stumbled sideways out of the bushes and fell on its side. The hair on the back of my neck stood up.

Oh my dear lord, no!

"I'm sorry!" I said to the disabled raccoon. "I shouldn't have left Laverne's cookies out here. It was my fault."

I glanced around, wild-eyed as a murderer, hoping no one else had seen.

"You must be Val," a voice said.

I nearly jumped out of my skin.

I whirled back around. About six feet away was a skinny old woman eying me from beneath a head full of curlers made from toilet-roll tubes. She was perched atop the saddle of an adult-sized tricycle. Soldered onto the front end, in lieu of a third wheel, was a metal grocery-shopping cart.

"I'm Charlene," she said, and waved. "Howdy! Just stoppin' by to see if you need anything. I'm headin' up to Junior's Save 'n' Stuff."

I couldn't for the life of me form a coherent word, much less a sentence.

"Admirin' my 'shopper chopper,' eh?" She grinned. "Stumpy fixed it up for me real nice, don't you think?"

"Yes," I managed.

"Junior's got a sale goin' on today. Two-fer-one on Cheetos and moon pies. You want you some, sugar?"

The angle of my vision shifted up and down slightly. I must have been nodding my head.

"All-righty, then. Got you down for both." Charlene grinned and pedaled off down the narrow dirt lane like a hillbilly remake of *The Wizard of Oz*— on LSD.

Okay. That's it. I'm done here.

I ran back inside the RV and slung everything hanging out of my suitcase back inside and clicked the fasteners. Thank goodness I hadn't unpacked yet. I'd spent too much time cleaning the kitchen and bathroom to have gotten around to disinfecting the chest-of-drawers.

As I scooted past the refrigerator, I didn't even hesitate.

Too bad, carrot sticks. You're on your own.

I flung my suitcase down the rickety metal steps and locked the RV behind me. But after I'd drug all my stuff over to Maggie, my alter ego got the best of me.

If you're going to be a writer, you need to toughen up, Val. I mean, this place is chock full of interesting characters, right?

A mosquito the size of a dragonfly landed on my arm.

Screw that!

I swatted it away, and scrounged around my purse for my car keys.

Where were they?

Dread filled my mind. They weren't in the RV. Either I'd lost the keys in the yard...*or I'd locked them in the trunk last night!*

Crap on a cracked-up cracker!

I straightened my shoulders, set my jaw to Valliant Stranger mode, and dragged my luggage back inside the RV.

Like it or not, I was here to stay.

Chapter Twelve

"Come on, Tom! Can't you come over *now* with the spare keys?" I pleaded over the phone.

"I wish I could. But it's almost rush hour. The traffic will be killer. It'll take me three hours minimum to get there. Not counting the drive back."

"I'm not worth it?"

"Val! You know I've got regional meetings all this week. Tonight I've got to schmooze a couple of bigwigs in town. I just can't make it happen. Sorry."

"Crap."

"But I tell you what. I'll get the keys overnighted to you when I get home from work today. You should have them by tomorrow afternoon, tops."

"Tomorrow? That means I'll be stuck here for another night!"

I could almost hear Tom smirk over the phone. "Come on, Valliant Stranger. Think of it as a...*literary adventure*."

"There's nothing literate about this place, Tom. And I'm afraid—"

"Listen," Tom interjected. "For the *last* time, there's no such thing as Bigfoot. And even if there was, I doubt he'd be into snickerdoodles. Especially not Laverne's. Give me the address and I'll get the keys off to you tonight. Honestly, that's the best I can do."

"I know," I conceded. "But I'm worried about using UPS. I don't think even the AARP can find this place."

"Why not?"

"Well, like I told you. It's in the middle of nowhere. The sign is falling down. And the community mailbox is a microwave stuck on a fence post with duct tape."

I waited a minute while Tom composed himself.

"Come on, Val," he finally managed between snorts. "You're a big girl. You can make it another night on your own."

I bit my lip. Part of me wasn't sure I could. But I wasn't about to admit that to Tom. My jaw clamped down on my molars.

"You're right, Tom. Just forget it. I'll figure some way out of here on my own."

I clicked off the phone. Tom tried to call back, but I didn't pick up.

Southern pride was an idiotic and enigmatic force not to be reckoned with lightly.

FOR THE NEXT HOUR, my phone buzzed every ten minutes or so, but I didn't dignify it with an answer.

I knew better.

Stuck in a dilapidated RV with nothing but lettuce and kale crisps for sustenance, things had nowhere to go but *ugly*. Tom's refusal to come to my rescue had pushed me over the threshold to hangry—a state in which anyone who knew me feared to tread.

In an attempt to appease myself, I fixed a snack, sequestered my phone safely inside a zipped pocket in my purse, and plopped down in the tiny dinette booth.

It was time to write.

I opened my laptop and clicked the start-up button. As I waited for it to boot up, I pulled the chain on the blinds and stared at my angry reflection in the RV's dusty window.

I bet Jorge's gorgeous girlfriend Sherryl isn't munching on a carrot stick right now like a dang gerbil.

I opened the file marked *Five Unique Ways to Kill Someone.*

I added another entry to my list; Cyanide Snickerdoodles.

The rhythmic movement of my fingers across the keyboard stimulated an old, entrenched habit that had lain dormant in my brain for years. Like a sprouting seed, I felt a smile slowly curve across my lips as my fingers moved. An automatic response akin to riding a bicycle fell into place in my mind, just as it had all those years ago.

Before Germany.

When I'd been a bona fide copy writer.

A newfound urgency pressed down on me. I closed *Five Unique Ways to Kill Someone* and opened a new file. I entitled it, *The Snicker-doodle Murders.*

A devious expression possessed my face like a lesser demon, and, as if by magic, my fingers began to fly across the keyboard.

I laughed to myself.

Who would have ever thought that a lack of pickles and a visceral dread of going outside would team up to become the muses that would kick-start my new writing career?

I WAS JUST TYPING "THE End" on a rough draft of my homework assignment, *The Snickerdoodle Murders,* when something scurried across my bare foot.

It had to have been either a mouse or a Florida-sized cockroach.

Anyone who'd ever seen a palmetto bug could understand why I was hoping for a mouse. My mouth flew open and ejected a high-pitched tone that made my own eardrums pop.

My knees nearly collided with my chin as I scrambled out of the booth. I shot a death stare at the plate littered with orange roots and dark-green leaves. Snacks I'd left untouched on the table.

This is what I get for filling this stupid RV with rodent food!

The mouse was the last straw. It truly was time to get out of this place. In a last-ditch effort to find my car keys, I grabbed my purse, turned it upside down, and shook its contents onto the dinette table.

A lipstick and two pens tumbled out and rolled off the table onto the booth seat. Crumpled receipts and papers fell like giant flakes of dandruff and covered the plate of carrots and seaweed.

I rifled through every pocket and crevice of my handbag.

No keys.

I turned my attention to the rest of the RV.

I grabbed a broom and swept the kitchen floor and around the cabinets. Still no keys.

I got on my knees on the bedroom floor and raked under the bed with the broom. My efforts resulted in one nudie magazine, an empty bag of pork rinds and what I hoped were the fossilized remains of five Milk Duds. I was sweeping them into a dustpan when someone rapped on the door.

I padded over and opened it.

Before I could say "Howdy," shopper-chopper chick Charlene pushed her curler-headed self inside, her arms laden with moon pies and Cheetos.

"How's it goin', Val?" she asked, and plopped the boxes and bags of processed foods, aka nectar of the gods, onto my tiny kitchen counter.

Drool began to fill in the space under my tongue.

"Uh. I'm doing okay. What do I owe you, Charlene?"

"Seven dollars and thirty-two cents. Moon pies ain't as cheap as they used to be."

I grabbed my wallet and counted out the bills while Charlene's wandering eyes took in every square inch of the tiny RV.

"What you been doin' all day?" she asked. Her curious, dark-brown eyes conveyed a tinge of suspicion.

"Nothing much," I said, and handed her a five and four ones. "What's there to do around here, anyway?"

"Lots. If you got a good imagination. Hey, this here's too much," she said as she counted the money.

"Keep it. For a delivery fee."

A smile cracked her pinched face.

"How's about I take you on a little tour of the place?"

"Uh...sure." I put my wallet back in my purse. "Hey. You don't happen to know a locksmith, do you?"

Charlene eyed me up and down. "Sure do. Woggles can get into darn near anything. What you want opened?"

"I think I locked my keys in the trunk."

"You don't say. Huh. I'll give him a ring. He just lives next door, you know."

Charlene's eyes continued their curious scanning as she reached into one of the huge pockets adorning her faded sack dress at hip level. She pulled out a cellphone. It looked as out of place in her hand as a wristwatch on a plesiosaur.

"You know, you're lucky," she said as she tapped the phone screen with a knobby finger. "Cell phone reception's sketchy around here. You got one of the good spots."

"Huh," I grunted, and forced myself to keep my hands off the moon pies.

"Woggles," Charlene said into the phone. "You busy? New gal locked her keys in the trunk. Okay. Good. Bye."

Charlene waggled her eyebrows at me and clicked off the phone. "He'll be right over."

A moment later, the RV door flew open and an old man's grey head poked its way inside like a snake in a coon-skin cap. The varmint's banded tail hung off Woggles' furry headpiece and trailed down his long neck like a mangy ponytail.

But that wasn't the most disconcerting thing about him.

Woggles had a lazy eye that was so off-kilter it was hard to nail down where to focus when I looked at him. I smiled at his left eye, only to watch it droop over to one side as if he were trying to glimpse his own ear. I tried the other eye.

"Hi. I'm Val," I sputtered.

"Wally Walters," he said. "Only you can call me Woggles, on account a my eye."

"Oh," I said, as if I hadn't noticed.

Woggles glanced around the RV, but made no attempt to come further inside or to reach out a hand to shake. Instead, he remained sandwiched in the crack in the door, a disembodied head wearing a dead animal for a hat.

"Nice to meet you, Woggles. So, do you think you can get into my car trunk?"

An arm snaked its way inside the RV toward his head. In its hand was a dark-red apple. Woggles bit a giant chunk out of it like Quasimodo munching on a crisp, human heart. The hand disappeared out the door again. Woggles chewed with cheeks puffed out like a greedy chipmunk.

"Sure thang," he said. Fragments of apple accompanied his words and spewed out across the floor like damp confetti.

"Woggles, you're always makin' a dad-burned mess with them apples," Charlene scolded. "Why don't you eat some *real* food?" She nodded toward the Cheetos on the counter.

"Charlene," Woggles said, "my momma tol' me an apple a day keeps the doctor away. She lived to be ninety-four. I figure at my age, I gotta eat five or six a day to keep them greedy varmints off a' my hide."

The snake arm appeared again, holding the gnawed apple. Woggles focused his good eye on it.

"These here apples sure beat the heck out of broccoli." He took another bite, tucked it in his cheek and said, "So, y'all ready to do this?"

I looked over at Charlene, then back at Woggles. "Sure."

Woggles' head disappeared.

Charlene pushed the door open. I followed her outside.

As I walked down the rickety steps, I could see Woggles was already hunched over behind Maggie's back end. When I rounded the side of the car, it became clear that Woggles' entire locksmith kit consisted of a wire coat hanger and a crowbar.

He hung the coat-hanger around his neck and steadied his grip on the crowbar.

"No!" I yelled. "I mean...wait a minute. I don't want to...damage the car."

Woggles eyed me funny. I think. It was impossible to be sure.

"Yore purty particular for a gal with a dirty seat."

Both of my hands flew to my butt cheeks.

Woggles smirked and nodded toward my car. He'd been talking about Maggie. I'd forgotten all about the muddy raccoon brawl that had taken place in her front seat last night.

"Oh. Well, it's just that...uh...I already called my boyfriend," I fumbled.

My hands fidgeted while my ears burned.

"He's mailing me the keys. You know, on second thought, if you don't mind, I'll just wait for the keys to get here. But thanks anyway for your offer, Woggles. What do I owe you for your time?"

Woggles shrugged. "Whatever."

As I ran inside the RV to grab some money from my purse, I thought about my "emergency" towel. I'd kept the stained-up old towel in Maggie's trunk "just in case."

This morning, I'd found the towel stuck to the Velcro on the bottom of my suitcase like a burr on a dog's hide. It had tagged along last night as I'd made a mad dash inside before the bush monster got me. I figured it would be perfect for wiping down Maggie's dirty seats. I grabbed it and my wallet and headed out the door.

"Thanks for your help," I said as I slapped a fiver in Woggle's hand.

He looked pleased, I think.

I turned to Charlene for a matching set of eyes to lock onto.

"Uh…how about you give me that tour now?" I asked, and tossed the old towel into Maggie's driver's seat.

"Be happy to," she said. "Foller me."

Chapter Thirteen

"I've never seen anything like it," I muttered absently as I stared at the concrete swimming pool. Only its kidney shape remained recognizable from the photos I'd seen of it on the Shell Hammock website.

Smack dab in the center of the pool's empty, cracked shell was the rear chassis of a long-bed pickup truck. Whether it had been placed there intentionally or was the result of a drunken miscalculation, I couldn't say. But the good folks at the Hell'ammo had made the most of it nonetheless.

While the cab end of the pickup had gone on to some other fate of which I had no knowledge, the truck *bed* was enjoying its retirement years with new purpose. It had been stripped of its wheels and lined with a blue plastic tarp, patched more times with silver duct tape than I could count.

A green garden hose snaked its way from around the back of an abandoned Cadillac carcass and into the truck bed. Water poured from it, slowly filling the makeshift swimming pool.

Sweat trickling down my back made the scene more tempting than I thought possible.

"The water looks nice and clear," I offered.

"Yep," Charlene said and folded her arms as if she was satisfied with the quality of the workmanship. "Gettin' her all fixed up for the fish fry tonight."

I wiped sweat from my upper lip and glanced longingly at the pool. Then I had second thoughts.

Surrounding the truck bed, like a gang of shiftless loiterers, was an odd assortment of mismatched chairs, ranging from a couple of bent-legged, metal folding chairs and a wicker rocking chair, to a gut-sprung naugahyde Barcalounger.

I closed my eyes and tried to convince myself that one of the seats wasn't an avocado-hued commode.

"Whad'ya think?" Charlene asked.

"Nice. I can't wait to give it a try," I said, uncertain if I actually meant it or not.

I diverted my attention to a flat-roofed, concrete-block building that reminded me of a campground toilet. "What's that building for?"

"That there's the clubhouse," Charlene explained. "Wanna take a peek inside?"

"Why not."

I wasn't sure if the Hell'ammo was growing on me or if Stockholm Syndrome was taking hold. "Appalled" and "intrigued" were having a fist fight in my gut, and to my surprise, "intrigued" was gaining the upper hand.

Charlene opened a plain, wood-paneled door that was peeling at the bottom and led me down a hallway past a couple of restrooms labeled Inboards and Outboards.

At the end of the hall, we entered a thirty-foot square concrete box of a room with no windows. She flicked on a light switch. Against the far wall was an eight-foot long wooden box. It contained a built-in console TV and a stereo turntable.

I'd seen one like it in my grandma's parlor when I was six. She'd been ironing and listening to a radio program. I remembered it quite clearly because it had scared the bejeezus out of me. I'd thought the radio announcer was a man trapped inside that coffin-like box.

I was still not one-hundred-percent convinced that it wasn't.

On top of the 1960's-era console sat a large, plasma-screen TV and the world's last functioning eight-track player. The tape at the top of the heap was *Pat Boone's Greatest Hits*.

If all that wasn't odd enough, what I saw next caused me to inhale sharply.

Positioned around the room and staring at the black screen like a lost, post-apocalyptic zombie tribe, was a random collection of bucket seats stripped from abandoned vehicles. I thought I recognized the emblem of a late-model Buick and a '70s-era Mustang.

"Nice," I said.

If I was in prison. In a third-world country.

Charlene shrugged. "It ain't much. But it's paid for."

I tilted my head and nodded. "Well, there's always *that*."

"Thursday's movie night," Charlene said. "*Gumball Rally*."

"Oh. What did you play last week?"

"*Gumball Rally*."

"Thanks. I'll keep that in mind."

As Charlene closed the clubhouse door behind us, I noticed a plastic lawn chair hanging from a tree by two ropes, as if it had been dealt a double helping of vigilante justice.

"What's that?"

"Tree swing," Charlene said. "Ain't you never seen one afore?"

"It's been a long time."

Charlene grinned. "Give her a try."

I walked over and inched my butt into the chair. I kicked off backward, but before I even made the arc to descend, the brittle chair cracked in half. Centrifugal force sent me tumbling, butt-first, into the dirt ruts scuffed out by the fools that had dared come before me.

Charlene came running up, her toilet-tube curlers jiggling.

"You all right, honey?" she asked.

I got up and dusted off my behind.

"Yeah. I'm okay."

I shot a perturbed glance at the mangled shards of plastic still swaying on their hangman ropes. "That thing should come with a warning."

Charlene's lip curled upward. She tutted. "Well, maybe things *have* gone a tad ramshackle around here since we lost Woody, our resident handy man."

"Right."

That explains why my showerhead is a beer can with holes punched in it.

"How long ago was that?"

"A month ago Sunday."

"Why'd he leave?"

"The Lord called him home."

"Oh. Sorry."

Charlene shrugged and adjusted the bobby-pin on a loose toilet roll.

"It happens."

AFTER THE STARS CLEARED from my eyes and my tailbone quit throbbing, Charlene and I continued down the dirt lane.

At the end of it sat a small trailer surrounded by the largest collection of wind-powered whirly-gig yard art I'd ever seen. A gust of wind sent them all swirling like propellers. I half expected the trailer to lift off and sail away on the world's tackiest magic carpet.

One flailing doohickey in particular caught my eye. It was a wooden squirrel whose tail twirled maniacally as its head tipped and appeared to take a bite from a plastic ear of corn.

I shook my head in wonder.

What kind of mind does it take to come up with something like that?

"What are you looking at?" a woman's voice snarled from inside the darkened trailer.

I gasped as if I'd been caught red-handed.

Charlene laughed.

"Who's that?" I whispered.

"Oh, that's just crabby old Elmira. Don't pay her no minds. She's a crafter. Keeps to herself, mostly."

"Crafter? As in *witch*craft?"

Charlene shot me a look that made me question my own sanity.

"What you talkin' about? Elmira ain't no witch! She makes new stuff outta old stuff, mostly."

"Oh, of course," I said as if I understood what that meant.

"Y'all quit starin'!" the voice called out again.

"Nobody's lookin' at you, Elmira," Charlene called back. "Listen here, Val. I heard it might come up a rain later on this afternoon. If'n it does, we'll have to move the fish fry to tomorrow. Well, I guess I better be gettin' back to my chores."

"Yeah, me too," I said, and shook Charlene's hand. "Thanks for the tour."

As I wandered back toward Number Thirteen, I collected an old bucket I found along the way. Back at the RV, I filled it with water and dishwashing soap, then cleaned Maggie's seats with my "emergency" towel.

It took a half an hour and two changes of water, but I got the seats looking decent enough. Satisfied with my work, I rinsed the muddy towel and hung it on the makeshift clothesline someone had strung between the RV's awning and a tree branch. Somehow, the dirty old rag looked right at home.

Maggie was clean, but with the possibility of more raccoons on the prowl and thunderstorms on the way, I needed to get her sealed up. Problem was, I couldn't close her convertible top without the keys.

Dang. What would McGyver do?

I decided to ransack the RV and see what my options were. It not being much bigger than Maggie, the search didn't take long.

Up on the top shelf of the bedroom closet, I found my solution. I covered Maggie up with a gunmetal-grey tarp, and duct-taped it to her side panels. I had no idea whether McGyver would have done the same thing, but I felt pretty confident that my neighbors would approve.

I stood back and admired my handiwork as I twirled the roll of duct tape in my hand like a fancy gunfighter in an old Western.

I was Valliant Stranger. And I was ready for anything.

Chapter Fourteen

What a difference a dessert could make.

After a sensible salad for lunch, I had a rendezvous with a romance novel and five banana moon pies. They'd proven just the ticket to help dissolve my anger and disappointment with Tom.

So what if Tom didn't drop everything and run to my rescue with my car keys? I was making do just fine without his help, thank you very much.

The comingling of sugar and grease in my gut had created the perfect salve to soothe my savage beast. So much so that, by late afternoon, I felt fairly certain that I could check Tom's text messages without spewing black thoughts into the world like an exploding oil rig.

My cellphone was still tucked safely inside the zipped pocket of my purse, despite my throttling the poor handbag until it had spilled its guts on the dinette table. I pulled the phone out and clicked "Tom."

The first text from him read: "Where do you keep your spare keys?"

Fifteen-thousand pounds of pressure per square inch bore down upon my molars. I snatched another moon pie out of the box.

"*Really*, Tom?" I growled as I tore open the cellophane wrapper. "They're on the freakin' key hanger beside the back door. You know, *that place where we hang all the keys?*"

I took a savage bite of moon pie, severing it in half. As my teeth pulverized the crumbly, sticky goodness, I took a moment to contemplate the male species in general.

What is it with men, anyway? They have no problem finding your hidden stash of candy in a shoebox in the closet, but they can't locate a set of keys hanging right in front of their noses?

I clicked on the second text. A jet of air streamed from my pursed lips.

It simply read: "Val?" The third read: "Hello?" The fourth: "Are you there?" The fifth: "I'm serious." The sixth: "Are you okay?"

I plopped down in the dinette booth and swept aside the spilled contents of my purse with a wave of my forearm. Elbows on the table, my fingers pecked out a reply text: "The keys are on the key rack by garage door, Boy Wonder."

I sucked the moon pie dregs from between my teeth and backspaced over "Boy Wonder." As I did, my elbow bumped my laptop. The screen blinked back to life. I'd forgotten to turn the dang thing off.

Crap! My files!

I dropped my phone and grabbed the computer. After punching in the code to unlock the screen, it opened onto the short-story I'd named *The Snickerdoodle Murders*. I scanned through the document. It appeared to be intact.

Whew!

I hit "save," closed the file and turned off the computer.

The clock above the stove read 4:38. I suddenly became aware of its loud ticking. It echoed through my tin-can abode, seeming to make each second pass slower. I drummed my nails on the laminate tabletop.

What should I do now? Take another stroll around the banana plantation?

I glanced at the collapsed carcass of my emptied purse. It lay in the booth beside me like a gutted fish. I grabbed it and stuck my wallet inside the pocket designated for it. My hairbrush went into the pocket beside that. I scrounged my lipstick and pens from the opposite bench and dutifully clipped them in place in the loops provided.

The sight of everything looking all neat and tidy caused a ridiculous, smug feeling of accomplishment to shoot through me. I scoffed at myself.

So much pride over nothing. This must be how a man feels that one time he actually replaces the empty toilet roll.

I reached for my tube of hand lotion. Something shiny and metallic glinted from underneath the heap of papers and crumpled old receipts littering the table. My heart flinched.

My keys!

My hand lurched into the pile of papers. Something stung me like a bee.

"Yow!"

I jerked my hand back. At the end of my middle finger, a crimson drop of blood glistened. My mind scrambled.

Snake!

My butt was out of that booth faster than a spider on a space shuttle.

I jettisoned across the kitchen and grabbed a wooden spoon hanging on the wall by the stove. Staying out of striking distance, I leaned over and stuck the spoon under the papers and flipped them over.

Lying underneath them wasn't a rattlesnake *or* my keys. Instead, it was that stupid Donut Shack VIP badge. The dang pin on it had pricked my finger. It figured. Donuts always *had* been my downfall.

I collapsed back into the booth with a thud. As I sucked on my injured finger, something else caught my eye. It was the pile of letters I'd pulled from the trash when I'd been tailing Goober at the post office the other day.

I thumbed through them. One was a blue envelope addressed to "Current Resident." It contained a pack of discount offers from neighborhood businesses. I wondered if there were any coupons for Depends in there, then wished I hadn't.

The next was a letter from the AARP. It was addressed to Gerald Jonohhovitz, aka Goober. I snorted. It seemed *no one* could escape the AARP's clutches, no matter how off the grid they were.

Goober hadn't opened the envelope, but it bore a familiar, greasy stain. I recognized it as the telltale, sticky-finger residue caused by Winnie's world-famous peanut-butter donut bombs. If asked to explain how I knew this in a court of law, I would've most definitely incriminated myself beyond all hope of leniency. Still, a self-congratulatory smile crept across my lips at my "Sherlock-Holmes-like" powers of deduction.

I tossed the AARP letter on the table along with the coupons and glanced at the next piece of paper. It was a check stub from Griffith & Maas. I saw the payout amount and shook my head. Minimum wage was definitely a soul-sucker.

I set the stub on top of the AARP envelope and looked at the last scrap of paper.

My jaw fell to the ground like a bad girl's drawers.

It was another paystub, smeared with the same greasy thumbprint as the others. Goober's name wasn't on the stub. Neither was any company name. The stub read simply, "For services rendered." It was in the amount of ten-thousand dollars.

What in blue blazes? What could Goober have done to earn that *kind of money?*

A sharp rap on the RV door made me nearly jump out of my skin. I glanced to my left. A pinched face stared at me through the oval of glass in the door.

"Fish Fry is on!" Charlene yelled through the pane. "See you at six o'clock!"

I nodded absently, but my mind was on something else...

...ten-thousand dollars!

I stared at the stub again. This had to be some kind of mistake. Goober didn't have any skills that could earn him that kind of dough.

Not unless I was highly mistaken about the going rate for a professional fart slinger. And he didn't have any family that could lend him the loot, either. I mean, I *guess* he didn't. I'd never really asked....

I turned the stub over. The other side was blank.

"For services rendered," I muttered. That didn't sound like it was for any kind of inheritance.

Wait a second. Goober was always cooking up some new get-rich scheme. Had he finally done it? Naw...

As far as I knew, Goober had nothing of value to sell...unless he'd pre-sold his body to science.

Had Goober taken a loan out on his carcass? Was his cadaver to be collected upon his death like one of those reverse-mortgage schemes? I mean, what other options were there?

I glanced at the clock. It was 5:11. I bit my lip and shoved the papers back into my purse. I'd have to deal with Goober later. At the moment, I had more pressing problems on my mind.

A good Southern woman wouldn't be caught dead showing up to a social gathering empty-handed, no matter how stringently her host had insisted that she do just that.

I needed to bring *something* with me tonight. But *what?*

One thing was for certain. If I went to that fish fry bearing a platter of kale chips, all rules regarding the reciprocation of said Southern hospitality would be instantly declared null and void.

In other words, things could get ugly for me.

Hmmm.

I tapped a finger on my chin. Aspiring mystery writer and redneck double-agent Valliant Stranger has just been handed her second major challenge of the day....

Waterproofing Maggie with duct tape and a tarp had been a piece of cake. The stakes inherent in this second puzzle were considerably more complicated.

I scanned the meager offerings in my RV's tiny kitchen. I was going to have to get creative...and tread carefully.

In the South, adhering to unspoken societal obligations often proved tricky like this. But thanks to my upbringing in Greenville, my family had provided me with a first-rate education on the care and feeding of hungry hillbillies. That's why I knew kale was definitely not on that menu.

MY TOES SCRUNCHED AS they tried to grip the wobbly cooler I was balanced atop. I shone a flashlight into the long, narrow cabinet above the two-burner stove. The glint of glass caught my eye. I reached deep into the cupboard and pulled out a wayward jar of spaghetti sauce.

Dang. What could I do with that?

I didn't have so much as a box of macaroni and cheese to go with it. I set the jar on the counter and shone the flashlight deep into the cabinet again. Finally, a bit of luck tumbled my way.

Now that's what I'm talking about!

I reached into the cupboard and teased the jar out until it was close enough to grab hold of.

I'd hit the redneck motherlode—a jar of marshmallow fluff.

My short-lived enthusiasm disappeared when I opened the jar. The fluff had shrunk down a good two inches from the top and was the consistency of Spam. I stabbed at it with a spoon and frowned. According to the expiration date, it had passed its prime a little over three years ago.

Crap on a cracker.

I sniffed the fluff anyway. It didn't smell funny...and it was still white...mostly. Besides, how could *marshmallow* go bad?

The gelatinous glob made a dull thud when I dumped it into a mixing bowl. The fluff had lost its...*fluff*. If I had a mixer, I reasoned I could beat it back into shape. But based on my prior pilfering through the

RV, I was absolutely certain there was no mixer, blender, or any other whirling contraption to be found.

Wait a second. Except for...

...a power drill! That could work!

I ran the three steps to the bedroom and grabbed the drill from the miniscule closet. Now all I needed was something to use as a beater. Something with a hole in it, like a slotted spoon.

I rifled through the only kitchen drawer. No dice. But there *was* a pair of scissors. It was worth a go.

I stuck the blade-end of the scissors into the bit shaft and flipped the switch on the drill. The scissors shot off, flew across the room, and stabbed a couch cushion through the heart.

"Ooops!"

I pulled the scissors out and covered the hole with another throw pillow. I stuck the blade-end back in the drill. Half a roll of duct tape later, those scissors weren't going anywhere.

I plunged my makeshift mixer into the bowlful of white goo, fired up the drill, and beat that marshmallow glop until the drill's battery gave up the ghost.

My chest puffed out and my eyes sparkled as I admired the gleaming bowl of merengue in front of me.

Like Lazarus, I'd brought the Stay Puft Marshmallow Man back to life. Or, at least, back to *fluff*.

Eat your heart out, McGyver.

Chapter Fifteen

"*The early evening shadows played upon the dish of Cheetos and marshmallow fluff in my arms, adding subtle highlights to the tangle of fluorescent orange worms writhing in a sea of sticky white goo.*"

Not bad for a first draft.

I named the file *Cheetos' Revenge*, saved it, and logged off my computer.

I was feeling pretty stoked. In just one day I'd finished a whole short story, started another, and had created a casserole from scratch. This whole "writer's retreat" thing was working out pretty well after all. Losing my keys had been a blessing in disguise. I'd actually accomplished something!

I closed the computer, grabbed the casserole, and headed out the door.

As I picked my way along the sandy lane toward the firelight flickering on the shore of Lake Rosalie, Deja-vu crept up behind me. Or was it just my imagination?

The odd blend of curiosity and trepidation wrestling in my gut felt so...*familiar*. I was sure I'd been in this situation before—another lifetime ago—on a dusty path just like this one. Maybe once upon a time I'd been a fur trapper, looking to make a peace offering to an indigenous tribe....

A chill wriggled down my spine like a daddy-longlegs spider.

Oh, no! What if my offering is rejected by the clan?

I looked down at the casserole. Orange fingers poked out from their shroud of white goo and pointed at me accusingly.

What if they saw the casserole as a joke...at their expense? What if they thought I was a jerk for bringing it?

An avalanche of doubt crushed my confidence. I tightened my grip on the casserole dish and hoisted it to my right. I was about to heave it into the bushes when a voice sounded behind me.

I was so startled I nearly yelped.

"Howdy, Val," Stumpy said as he walked up beside me. "Glad you came. Crowd's kind 'a sparse since the snowbirds flew on back home."

"Oh. Right. Thanks." I smiled sheepishly. "What should I do with this?" I shrugged, raising the casserole dish a few inches.

"Aww. I done tol' ya you didn't have to bring nothin.'"

"My momma would roll over in her grave if I didn't," I said, in a voice I barely recognized as my own. As if possessed by ghosts of the past, I'd reverted back to the Southern twang it had taken me thirty years to get shed of.

My face flushed with heat. I hoped it didn't glow in the dark.

"Put 'er over there."

Stumpy pointed a short finger toward the open tailgate of a rusty Chevy pickup. The truck had either been parked or abandoned next to a rusted-out washing machine.

"And grab yourself a cold one while you're over there," he added.

I set my odd offering down on the tailgate next to a platter of canned pear halves. Each lay on a lettuce leaf and sported a dollop of yellowing mayo where their pits used to be. Every ghostly pear was garnished with a few shreds of processed, yellow, cheese-like food product.

Next to the pears were bowls containing the obligatory potato salad, baked beans, and tub of green Jell-O, complete with canned fruit chunks floating around in it like suspended vomit.

Geez. This makes Winky's party look like a soiree at the Ritz.

I leaned over the old washing machine and grabbed a beer from the icy water in its rusty tub. I cracked it open and chugged half of it down before I headed over toward the others.

As I surveyed the odd collection of humanity sitting around the campfire, I felt an unexpected, interspecies connection I'd only felt once before—with a gorilla at the zoo. Maybe it was because my real mother once lived in an RV, too.

"I believe you done met Woggles," Stumpy said as I stepped up to the crowd.

He motioned for me to sit on an old dinette chair. Its vinyl seat had been pre-ripped for my inconvenience.

"Yes. Hi, Woggles," I said. He tipped his beer can at me in a silent salutation.

"This here's Slim," Stumpy said, and waved a short-fingered hand at a man who was anything *but* slender.

"Howdy," Slim said, and leaned his hairy, four-hundred pound frame forward like a grizzly bear.

The motion caused his inadequate dinette chair to groan in a way that made me wince. I shook his huge, beefy hand. It enveloped my own as if it were a newborn's.

"And I know you done met Charlene," Stumpy continued.

I nodded at the thin woman who rode around in a shopper chopper and made home deliveries. She'd changed into polyester slacks and a top encrusted with enough rhinestones to cover Cincinnati. Her silvery-blonde hair was beautifully coiffed in soft curls.

Huh. Who knew toilet-paper tubes could be so handy?

"You cain't rightly *not* know Miss Busybody," joked Woggles about Charlene. She smiled at me, then shot Woggles a dirty look.

"And hey, ever-body, this here feller's named Steve," our host Stumpy said. "He drove in just about an hour ago."

I looked Steve over. He was a tallish, white guy of indeterminate age and weight. He wore a ball cap over a shaggy head of dark hair. His goatee-like beard was equally unkempt. Accompanying it like one bad decision after another was one of those smarmy, pencil-thin moustaches that made me instantly suspect him of being dimwitted, involved in shady dealings, or, most likely, *both*.

Steve smiled, revealing a gold front tooth.

Hmmm. Apparently Steve was a man of means, relatively speaking.

"Hi Steve, I'm Val," I said, and extended my hand to shake. Steve didn't reciprocate. I gave him a bit of side-eye and took my seat.

"Well now, what say we get this here show on the road," Stumpy said.

"What about me!" a female voice bellowed from the bushes.

A short, squat woman in her late sixties emerged from the slate-colored darkness. Her blunt, boxy, gray bob looked as if she'd cut it herself. With a knife. In the dark. Her pudgy, square body was covered in a loose-fitting, faded house dress that fell just above her saggy knees.

She stomped over and wedged herself into the chair beside me with an indignant huff.

I waited a moment, then dared a sideways glance. Below her angry eyes and pursed lips, the woman sported a thin beard of curly white hairs. It resembled a loose wad of fishing line glued haphazardly to her chin. Possibly in the dark. With a knife.

"All right, then," Stumpy sighed. "Fire up the fryers, boys. Queen Elmira has arrived."

I WAS DOLING OUT A spatula of orange and white goop onto my plate when a man's voice sounded behind me. He was so close to me I could feel his breath on my neck.

"Don't tell me. Marshmallow and Cheeto squares?"

It was gold-toothed Steve.

I shrugged and offered a slightly embarrassed smile.

"You're pretty astute for a vagabond."

"Who you callin' an ass toot in a Vagabond?" a screechy woman's voice yapped. "You ain't no beauty queen, yoreself, Missy. Actin' all high and mighty. And you don't even own your own trailer!"

I turned around to face Elmira. Her crinkled nose and pursed lips told me she was sporting for a fight.

"Astute," I said.

She raised a flabby, white fist at me.

I took a step back and yelped, "Hold on!"

"Astute means smart," Steve said, stepping between us. "It was a meant as a compliment, Elmira. And I don't have a Vagabond. I've got a Winnebago."

"Oh," Elmira said. Her voice softened, but her face didn't. She continued to glare at me suspiciously. "Watch it with that high-brow talkin'."

"Okay," I said. "Here. Try one of these." I offered her the orange and white glop still hovering on the spatula.

Elmira snatched it and shoved a corner of it in her mouth. It disappeared along with her scowl.

"Don't you go trying to sweeten me up, neither," she said, but her face showed my ploy had worked. As she waddled off toward the campfire, Charlene joined us.

"What's up with her?" I asked. "Somebody steal her cruller?"

Charlene shot me a dirty look. "What do you mean by that?"

I flinched. "Nothing. She just reminds me of my own dear, sweet mother."

"Oh," Charlene said. "Well, just so you know, me and Elmira's sisters."

I bit my lip and nodded. "Family is family. Am I right?"

"Darn straight," Charlene said. A grin broke out on her face. "Gimme some of that." She pointed at my casserole. "I heard it was purty darn good."

I relaxed with relief. No harm, no foul. My casserole was a hit!

Steve grinned under his smarmy moustache as I served Charlene a square. As she headed back to the bonfire with her sweet treat, Steve took the spatula from my hand and served himself a piece.

"Huh. That's surprisingly good," he said, licking his fingers.

"The secret's in the marshmallow fluff," I bragged. "I came up with that myself. You see, I didn't have any marshmallows, except the gooey middles of some moon pies. I thought about using them, but I figured I'd better not. In Polk County, that might get me arrested for desecrating a local treasure."

Steve studied me for a moment. "I see you don't learn too quickly from your mistakes, do you?"

"What do you mean?"

"Open mouth, insert foot."

He demonstrated by opening his mouth and inserting more of the marshmallow and Cheeto glop.

I sneered. "Oh, don't be such an ass toot."

Steve laughed and choked on the mouthful of casserole. His hand flew up to his throat, and he got busy hacking out a lung.

"Are you okay? I asked, and slapped him on the back. I fished the last beer out of the washing machine and cracked the tab on it. Steve grabbed it out of my hand and poured it down his throat.

"Ever thang all right over here?" Woggles asked as he stumbled up.

"Yeah," Steve gasped.

Woggles' good eye scanned the empty washtub. "Dang. No more beer. Party's over. Guess I'll head home. I ain't feeling too good, noways."

"Can you see okay in the dark?" I blurted without thinking.

Geez! Steve's right. My mouth sure can hold a pile of feet.

"I'll be fine," Woggles said, and wandered off into the night.

"Them crazy eyes sees it all," Stumpy said, stepping out from the shadow Woggles left behind. "He don't miss much. Some folks 'round here thinks Woggle's is psychic, you know."

Stumpy reached around in the washtub for a beer and came up empty-handed. "Huh. Looks like it's closin' time."

"She used the last one to save my life," Steve said, his voice still raspy.

Stumpy laughed and slapped Steve on the back hard enough to make his eyes bulge. "Well, at least it went to a good cause."

"Thanks for inviting me, Stumpy," I said. "That was the best catfish and hush puppies I've had in like...*forever*."

"You don't say," Stumpy grinned. "Well, yore mighty welcome, young lady."

"I'm serious, Stumpy. Everything was delicious. And...thank you for...well, you all made me feel right at home."

"That's mighty sweet, Val."

Stumpy gave me a kind, fatherly smile. "I guess I'll get me another slice a that Cheeto pie and head home." He grabbed a square and looked Steve and me over. "Somebody ought to see you back to your place. Ain't fit for a purty woman like you to be wanderin' 'round alone in the dark."

Stumpy winked at Steve.

"Stumpy's right," Steve said. "A woman can't be too careful these days."

Before I could answer, Steve took me by the arm.

"Shall we?" he asked.

I looked at Steve, then back at Stumpy. An odd whirlwind of emotions swept through me. I was flattered, confused, and a little flabbergasted at being called a young lady. But the biggest shock was how much this place actually *did* feel like home.

I turned to Steve. "Uh...sure."

Stumpy smiled and kept a watchful eye on us as Steve and I ambled off toward my RV.

After we'd gotten out of earshot of everyone, Steve pulled my arm in tight, drawing me closer to him. "So, what's a nice gal like you doing in a place like this?"

"I'm married," I lied.

Steve laughed and loosened his grip. "So what are you doing out here all on your own?"

"Well, it's kind of a secret. But I'm working on a story."

"A story? Like a reporter? What's it about?"

"More like a novelist. And I don't know yet. You on vacation?"

"I guess you could say that."

The yellowish light emanating from my RV window looked as welcoming to me as a beacon to a drowning sailor. I pulled my arm out of Steve's.

"Well, thanks for seeing me home."

"You going to stay awhile?" he asked as I scurried to the door.

"I don't think so. You?"

"Depends."

"On what?"

"On which way the wind blows."

Steve turned and disappeared into the night. I got out my key and reached for the door.

As my fingers encircled the doorknob, they got tangled in something wrapped around it. I squinted in the dim light and made out the silhouette of a round object dangling from a string. I unhooked it from the knob and scooped it up in my hand. The fragrance of cinnamon wafted in the night breeze.

I held the trinket to my nose and sniffed it as I carried it inside.

Mmmm. How cute! Someone left me a little RV-warming present. Sure beats the smell of moth balls and mildew....

I flipped on the kitchen light and "cute" skittered out the window along with my smile. I heard a squeal shoot out my mouth, then my heartbeat as it pulsed in my ears.

Hanging from the string in my hand was a shriveled, shrunken head. Its grotesque face, rimmed in haggish moss hair, grinned maniacally at me with a set of sharp teeth made from broken shells.

"Aaarrghh!"

I flung the thing across the room. It ricocheted off the refrigerator and clanked into the sink. I shook my head, shuddered, then laughed nervously.

Come on, Val! A shrunken head? That can't be right.

I tiptoed over to the sink and peered inside. The thing was gone! How could that be?

The only thing in the sink was my dirty coffee cup. I noticed a clump of Spanish moss sticking out of the grey water inside it. Cautiously, I reached for the mug handle and dumped it out.

I gasped again. I hadn't imagined it.

Two beady, cat-like eyes stared at me from a shriveled face the color of dried tobacco. Clutched in the shrunken head's jagged teeth was a soggy piece of paper rolled up into a scroll.

I had to know what was written on that scroll!

But there was no use taking any chances. I subdued the shriveled head with a wooden spoon before warily plucking the paper from between its sharp little teeth.

As I unrolled the soggy scroll, a message scrawled in red ink appeared. It spread across the paper like a bloodstain, the last few letters not much more than a smear. It read:

Stay Away.

Chapter Sixteen

So much for "feeling right at home."

As I stared at the shriveled head, I became aware that I was aping its horrific expression as it glared back at me with sinister, cat-eyes and vicious, jagged teeth.

Even though the monstrosity was no bigger than a tangerine, my heart thumped in my throat. My imagination envisioned the head sprouting legs and coming after me like that disembodied eyeball from in that low-budget B movie.

No, sirree. This RV isn't big enough for the two of us.

I grabbed the wooden spoon, scooped up the hideous voodoo head with it, and catapulted it out the door and back into the dark, evil night from which it had come.

My skin crawled as I heard it thump onto the ground. I slammed the door, locked it, and shoved the cooler against the door for good measure. I hoped that would be enough. After all, I had no experience with shrunken heads and their devious ways.

With the unwelcome voodoo head duly thwarted, I collapsed into the dinette booth. I didn't know whether to laugh or cry.

What was this place, anyway?

Either I was cavorting with a bunch of nice country folks, or I was the next intended victim of a coven of blood-thirsty demons. I guess only time would tell.

No matter what, though, I knew I was in way over my head. I didn't want to admit defeat, but it was time to call Tom.

I lifted my cellphone from the table. The display lit up. On it was my text to Tom about the car keys being on the key rack. I'd forgotten to press "send."

Crap!

I clamped my teeth tighter than my Aunt Pansy's girdle and mashed the send button with all my might.

The phone cut out.

"Nooooo!"

I tried to turn it back on, but it wouldn't budge. Either I'd squashed its tiny brains out or the battery was dead. I pilfered through my suitcase and found the charger. I tried to stick it in the phone but it didn't fit. I must have picked up Tom's charger by mistake.

"You've got to be kidding me," I groaned aloud.

Crap on a cracker! This was all Tom's fault! His stupid stuff was spread all over my house...getting me all confused. Dang it! Why in the world did I let him move in?

I flung the charger across the RV.

Oh, how I wish Tom was here now....

My heart thumped hollow in my chest as I re-checked the deadbolt on the door and the locks on every single window. When I'd finished securing every one of the tiny RV's possible entry points, I brushed my teeth, washed my face and grabbed my spray bottle of Ty-D-Bol.

From my perch in the dinette booth, I kept a wary eye on that bloody note until the smeary red words, "Stay Away," were burned into my frazzled retinas.

A NOISE STARTLED ME awake in the middle of the night again. Apparently, the RV's manufacturer had spared every expense when it came to insulation. I would swear I could hear every cricket in Polk County chirping on my roof.

My head was slumped forward. My neck ached. As I lifted my head to look around, my vertebrae cracked like a long line of knuckles.

Ugh.

I was still in the dinette booth.

Groggily, I scooted across the booth and stood up. As I took a fumbling step toward the bathroom, I saw something move at the end of the hallway.

I froze like I'd been dipped in liquid nitrogen.

I willed my bleary eyes into focus. Out of the haze, the shadowy silhouette of an intruder stared back at me from inside the bedroom.

This can't be happening.

I blinked once. Twice. It was still there. Staring at me.

The hair on the back of my neck pricked up. The ghostly apparition didn't budge.

Holy crap! It's the demon spirit of that shrunken head! It's come to kill me!

"What do you want?" I croaked, my lungs so tight I could barely speak.

No reply.

In the silence, I could hear its heavy breathing. I took a step backward. The hideous intruder took a step.

Adrenaline pulsed through my veins, standing the rest of my hair on end.

I turned to run.

I only managed two steps before whatever it was caught me by the foot.

As I fell toward the floor, it bashed me hard on the back of my head. My face hit the linoleum, and just before everything went black, I saw a mouse staring at me from under the cabinet baseboard.

Chapter Seventeen

I woke up sopping wet in a pool of blood. My head throbbed with dull, intermittent pulses of pain. Sunbeams shot their cruel lasers through the kitchen window straight into my eyes, turning up the volume on my headache. I raised a sticky, red-stained hand to my forehead.

Memories of last night flooded back. I sat up with a start.

As my face rose from the floor, something dislodged from the side of my head and slid down my cheek. It plopped onto my shoulder, then fell into my lap. A pang of horror clamped my eyes shut.

Dear lord! Is that my ear? Have I been cut to pieces by some sick slasher?

I cracked opened one eye and peeked down. In between my knees, a plump, silver-haired man smiled back at me. His cook's hat, cocked at a rakish angle, seemed to imply that the whole thing had all been in jolly good fun.

I let out a half-cry/half-laugh and plucked the Chef Boyardee spaghetti sauce lid from my lap. I wasn't covered in blood. I was covered in spaghetti Bolognese.

I glanced around. So was the entire kitchen.

"Oh, great," I muttered.

I grabbed the end of the dinette table and pulled myself to standing. The dull ache pulsing between my eyes picked up tempo. I took a step with my right foot. My little toe shot a bullet of pain directly into my brain.

I looked down at my little toe. It was the size and color of a small plum.

What the? Why would someone break into my RV, knock me out with a jar of spaghetti sauce and smash my little toe?

A chill shot through me.

Oh no! What if they're still in here!

I leaned over and took a trembling, cautious peek down the hallway toward the bedroom.

My instincts had been right. The intruder was still there.

A hand came up and slapped me in the forehead. It was my own. Halfway down the hall, the bathroom door hung open. The intruder last night had been my own reflection in the full-length mirror.

I'd run away from my own shadow.

What an idiot!

Last night I'd stubbed my toe on the corner of the dinette booth. When I fell, it must have knocked the jar of spaghetti sauce off the table and right onto my dimwitted noggin.

Bloody. Freaking. Brilliant.

Great detective work, Val. You just solved the case of your own stupidity.

I STRIPPED OFF MY TOMATO-spattered clothes and stuffed myself inside the phone-booth sized shower. Last night's fried food fest hadn't done me any favors. My butt was already big enough to fill a bench. Now my stomach was as bloated as a dead toad-frog.

After I cleaned myself up, I put on a loose-fitting sundress, bandaged my toe and started in on the sauce-splattered kitchen.

Over by the fridge, I found the busted jar of spaghetti sauce. The expiration date revealed it had gone bad sometime during the second Bush administration.

Geez! The jar must have exploded on impact. That explains the spatter. That crap is everywhere!

I sponged down the sink, counters and cabinets and started on the booth. The mouse was gone, but it had left a trail of footprints across the table.

Gross!

With no mop to be found, I hobbled outside and yanked my "emergency" towel from the makeshift clothesline. I tried to wipe down the floor with it, but it was still so dirty from cleaning Maggie that I only managed to add mud to the Bolognese. Not a pretty combo.

I flung the towel out the door and got the one I'd just dried myself off with.

A half an hour later, every towel in the place was filthy and so was I. I took another shower and changed into jean shorts and a t-shirt.

My head had stopped throbbing, but my toe wasn't that easily dissuaded. To make matters worse, my tin-can condo was heating up in the late morning sun like an Easy-Bake oven fitted with a million-watt bulb.

I cranked the window-rattler AC unit down to sixty-eight degrees and hoped for the best. What I really needed, though, was a nice, cold drink.

I opened the freezer in search of ice. The tiny freezer was empty except for my flask of Tanqueray and a miniscule, Barbie-sized ice tray. I dumped the dehydrated, yellowed chips of ice into a glass. They looked like a pile of dead man's toenails.

Geez, Louise. Maybe I can borrow Charlene's shopper chopper....

I stuffed my sauce-soaked clothes and towels into a garbage bag, opened the RV door and tossed it outside. As I did, my eyes caught sight of Queen Elmira's back end.

She straightened up, turned around, and glared at me.

I couldn't decide what it was that was more disconcerting about that woman. Was it her bad attitude, her frizzy beard, or her belief that it was okay to wear a white sports bra as a top?

I waved at her. She shot me a look that could have melted a steel girder at the North Pole.

"Witch!" she hissed.

Dumbfounded, I stood in the doorway and watched her huff down the lane.

"Don't take it personal. Elmira hates near 'bout ever'body."

"Hi, Stumpy."

"Mornin' Val. You seen Woggles around here?"

"No. Not since last night. Hey, do you know where I can get some ice?"

"Up by the laundry-mat."

"There's a laundry here?"

"Sure. A dollar a load."

"Thanks. Good to know."

"You got quarters?"

"Yessir."

"All right then. You should be all set. You have yourself a good morning, young lady."

"You, too. And thanks again for inviting me to the fish fry last night. It was fun."

I went inside and pulled a roll of quarters from my purse. I always kept at least two full rolls in my handbag at all times. My adoptive mother, Lucille Jolly, had shown me by example that a purse full of quarters was the equivalent of a redneck hacky sack. It could come in handy against stray dogs, strange women, and wayward husbands. Over the years, I'd begun to see her point more and more.

Quarters in hand, I grabbed my writing notebook, locked the RV and slung the bag of towels over my shoulder. Barefoot and with a smashed toe, I hobbled down the dirt road in the general direction of the laundromat looking like a down-and-out Santa with a busted sleigh.

Chapter Eighteen

I don't know why I was so surprised, but I was. The Hell'ammo's so-called "laundromat" was just a derelict washer and dryer loitering under an open, tin-roofed porch like a pair of stray dogs.

Both appliances appeared to have been scabbed together from the remains of the poor machines that had come before them. I hobbled over to the washer, lifted the Harvest Gold lid on its otherwise white frame, and peered cautiously inside to make sure it wasn't already occupied.

Seeing as the washing machine didn't contain anyone else's laundry or a newborn litter of varmints, I bought some soap out of the small vending machine nailed to the wall, ripped the top off a box of Stain-Killer Tide about the size of a deck of cards, and poured it all in.

I hoisted the garbage bag up and let the Chef Boyardee-encrusted clothes and towels tumble in. The last thing to fall out was my muddy "emergency" towel. It was as stiff and black as a charred steak.

Beyond saving, I tossed it in the trash and pumped four quarters into a slot in the washer. Seeing as how there was no "post-apocalypse" wash option, I mashed the button for "heavy duty" and hit start. The machine jerked to life and began humming.

With thirty-five minutes to kill and a little toe that was screaming bloody murder, it didn't seem worth it to shamble back to the RV. So, I took advantage of the "waiting room" facilities instead. Of the two chairs sitting in the open yard amongst the debris, one looked as if it just might have enough strength left to hold my weight.

I limped over to the ice machine and blew seventy-five cents on a twenty-pound bag of ice, then plopped down in the dilapidated lawn chair.

As I sat there, a plastic bag drifted by like a tumbleweed, leaving me with an idea. I snatched the wayward bag and fashioned it into an icepack for my toe. That done, I hoisted my foot up to rest on the up-turned hull of a refrigerator, and gently applied the little bag of ice. The relief was instant.

"Aahh."

It seemed a shame to waste the other nineteen pounds of ice. A while back, I'd read an article about how ice could kill fat cells. Some scientist had come to that conclusion after noticing that kids who ate popsicles developed dimples.

If ice pops could put a divot in some kid's fat cheeks, why couldn't it carve out a sizable slab from my stomach? Besides, what did I have to lose? It was sweltering outside, and there was nobody around to tell me not to try this at home.

I hauled the bag of ice up onto my bloated gut and wondered how long it would take me to get down to a size six. While I waited for my fat to melt away, I got out my notebook and fiddled with more ideas on how to kill someone with a casserole....

"That's a novel way to cool off."

I looked up. Gold-toothed Steve was staring at me, an amused look plastered on his smarmy face.

"Yeah. I call it 'country cryosurgery.'"

Steve's bushy black eyebrows met in the middle. "What?"

"Never mind. What have you got there?"

"Oh. I saw you hobbling down the path. Thought you might could use this."

Steve handed me an upside-down push-broom. Its flat pad of bristles had been wrapped in a towel and secured with duct tape.

"What am I supposed to do with that?"

"It's a crutch. I made it myself."

"You don't say. What's with the round thingy halfway down the handle?"

"Drink holder. Thought it might come in handy."

"Oh. Sure," I laughed. "But it would be handier if it already had a drink in it."

Steve grinned. "I thought you might say that."

He reached in a plastic bag and pulled out a Fosters.

"My favorite!" I said.

"Beer. Never leave home without it. Trade you some of that ice for a sort-of cold one?"

"Deal."

I grinned, took the beer, and handed Steve the bag of ice from my lap.

"So, what's your story?" I asked as I cracked the tab.

Steve shrugged. "Not much to tell." He eyed my notebook. "What are you working on there?"

"If you must know, ingenious ways to get rid of a body."

Steve's eyebrows disappeared into his baseball cap. "Oh."

"It's an assignment for a class I'm taking."

"Let me guess. Mafia 101?"

I smirked. "No. But I like the way you think."

"Here here," Steve said, and lifted his beer for a toast.

I raised the beer to my lips and took a sip.

A high-pitched scream echoed through the trees.

Steve and I spewed our beer.

Steve gasped, glanced around, and looked at me. His expression seemed to register both concern and amusement.

"I didn't realize it was Bigfoot mating season."

My heart flinched. "You really think that was the call of the wild man?"

Steve opened his mouth to answer, but Stumpy came crashing out of the woods, rendering him mute. The old man hightailed it past us without saying a word.

Steve rubbed his goatee absently.

"Depends on your definition of a 'wild man.' But I have to say, Stumpy's rapid exit did seem rather ominous."

"Geez! Help me!" I cried as I tried to rock my butt out of the hole in the dilapidated lawn chair. "I'm a sitting duck!"

Steve tried to look serious, but I knew a stifled grin when I saw one.

"Don't worry," he said. "Here, take the crutch."

I hoisted myself up on the push-broom. The washing machine cut off.

"Please. Steve. Could you help me get my clothes out of there?" I nodded my head toward the washer.

"Really? A murderous beast is breathing down our necks and you're worried about your laundry?"

"It would be rude to leave it. What if someone else needed to use the washer?"

Steve shook his head. "You've got an odd set of priorities, Val."

I grimaced apologetically. "I blame my mother."

Steve snorted and lifted the lid on the washer.

"Who doesn't?"

BY THE TIME STEVE HELPED me hobble back to the RV, the Hell'ammo was eerily deserted. I stuffed the rest of the ice in my freezer and made Steve a gin and tonic to thank him. It was either that or kale chips.

When I stuck my head out the door of the RV, Steve was hanging up the last of my laundry on the old clothes line. Everything was flecked with telltale pink spots, compliments of Chef Boyardee.

"Crappy job," I said.

"And here I thought you'd be all grateful and what-not."

"Oh! Not you, Steve. I meant the washer!"

"Okay. That's better."

"Here. I made you something."

"I hope it's not another mess. I should be getting paid for being your domestic slave."

"Har har. No. It's a gin and tonic."

"Wage terms accepted."

I handed him his drink, hobbled back around to fetch my own, and joined him on the porch.

"Be honest. Do you think there's such thing as Bigfoot?" I asked as we sipped cocktails by the clothesline.

"I've seen stranger things."

"Like what?"

"Well, like *that*, for instance."

I glanced in the direction Steve nodded and did a double-take.

Coming up fast along the dirt path was a babushka-headed Charlene, peddling her shopper chopper for all she was worth. Inside her shopping cart, still in her sport bra and skirt, was her sister, Elmira.

The queen was on her knees in the cart, facing forward, her hair blowing around her head like a scraggly Medusa. She held a large wooden cross out in front of her, making her look like one of those patron saints carved on the bows of old Spanish galleons.

"Were they crying?" I asked as they whizzed by us, leaving a cloud of orange dust in their wake.

"I don't know," Steve muttered absently. "I wasn't looking at their eyes."

"I think we should go see what's going on."

"I dunno," Steve hesitated. "If a skunk ape really *is* after them, we don't stand a chance of outrunning them. Plus, it looks like they've got God on their side."

I laughed partly out of fear, and partly because of the utter absurdity of, well, *all of it*.

"All right. Let's go."

I limped alongside Steve as he traced Charlene's chopper marks all the way to the clubhouse. A crowd was gathered around the edge of the pool.

"What happened?" I asked Stumpy. He didn't answer.

I hobbled over on my broom crutch and peered around his shoulder. The air went out of me like a punctured tire.

Inside the makeshift truck-bed pool, a body floated, face up. One eye stared blankly skyward. The other, well...didn't.

Chapter Nineteen

Woggles was dead.

Dread stabbed my heart. But it wasn't all for Woggles. Floating in the water beside him was the bottom half of a plastic container. Inside it, like the lone survivor in a doomed life raft, was the crescent-shaped remains of a half-eaten snickerdoodle.

My heart sunk to my knees.

Oh dear lord. Laverne's cooking has finally gone and killed someone.

My legs grew wobbly. I felt light-headed and woozy. The world started swaying. I leaned into the crutch, then crumpled to the ground like a soggy bag of Stumpy's boiled peanuts.

WHEN I CAME TO, I WAS lying on the pool deck. Woggles was splayed out on a stretcher beside me. Everyone from the trailer park was gathered around us like curious, poorly-dressed vultures.

I shot up to sitting.

"I'm not dead!" I cried out, feeling the need to prove the point.

"I think we got that," an EMT said, then spoke into his radio. "She's awake, Chief."

"What happened?" I asked.

"You passed out," Steve said, and showed me his gold-toothed grin.

"Oh." I looked over at my not-so-lucky companion. "Poor Woggles."

"Here. Let me help you up."

Steve stretched out a hand. I took it. He pulled me up to standing, then handed me the broom-crutch. Charlene and Elmira eyed us warily as I steadied myself on my feet. I took a tentative step.

"Don't go anywhere," the EMT barked.

"What? Why not?" I asked.

"Chief wants to talk to you."

"Chief?"

"That would be me," said a middle-aged man in a police uniform. He broke through the small crowd and stepped to within a foot of me. "Chief Earl Collins."

"Oh," I said. "Mr. Collins—"

"*Chief* Collins," he said. "And *you* are?"

"Sorry, *Chief* Collins. I'm Val Fremden."

"Tell me, Ms. Fremden, what do you think happened here?"

I thought about Laverne's cookies. Had they done old Woggles in? A frog tied a knot in my tonsils.

"I...uh...I don't know."

"Hmmm. Well, that's too bad."

"What do you mean, Chief?"

"It means we're gonna have to do this the hard way."

I shifted my weight on the crutch. "I don't understand."

"Look around," he said. "According to everybody here, you killed Wally Walters."

"What?!" I scanned the faces of my accusers. Their eyes darted around like minnows in a pond.

"But...but..." I stuttered.

"Um...Chief?" Steve said, holding up a finger. "Just for the record, that would be everyone but *me*."

"Have it your way, mister. You can come in for questioning, too."

Steve's eyes doubled in size.

"Well," he backtracked, "I didn't say she *didn't* do it."

"Right," Chief Collins said. "Ms. Fremden, I'd like you to accompany me down to the station."

Oh, dear lord!

"Are you going to...cuff me?"

Chief Collins looked surprised. "Do I need to?"

"No, sir."

"Well, all right then. You have some ID on you?"

"It's back at the RV."

"Lead the way."

I hobbled down the dirt path. Chief Collins lagged a few yards behind me and talked to a man holding a clipboard.

"What do we have so far?" I heard Chief Collins ask.

"First blush, it looks like foul play," the man answered. "Wounds to the body suggest a possible knife attack."

Geez. I never thought I'd be relieved to hear those *words.*

"...or he could have been poisoned."

I stumbled and nearly fell.

"Are you all right up there?" Chief Collins asked.

I didn't dare look back. I'd never been good at hiding a guilty face.

"Sure. Uh...this is my RV."

I fished the key from my pocket, limped up the steps and opened the door.

"Mind if we take a look inside?" the man with the clipboard asked.

"No. Not at all."

The two men made quick work of surveying the inside of my tiny RV. By the time I'd gathered up my purse and inched my swollen toe into some flip-flops, they were through.

"Everything okay?" I asked.

Chief eyed me with suspicion.

"Not particularly. Looks like signs of a struggle," he said, and nodded his head toward the bedroom. My suitcase looked like it had exploded in there.

"Oh. No struggle. That's all me. I'm just...a bit of a slob, you might say."

"What happened to your toe?"

"Well, I—"

"Chief, take a look at the ceiling," clipboard man said. He pointed his pencil at a few dark-red specks. "Looks like blood splatter."

"People always forget about the ceiling," Chief Collins said, and tutted as his eyes met mine. "Evidence of a cleanup in the sink, too, Rogers. Get some samples for testing."

"But...it's not what you think," I said lamely.

"You don't say," Chief Collins said.

I smiled weakly. "Well, it's kind of a funny story, really. I can explain—"

"I'd appreciate it if you would do just that, Ms. Fremden. But not here. Down at the station. Into a tape recorder. Rogers?"

The man with the clipboard said, "I'm on it, sir."

AS DETECTIVE ROGERS shut the back door on the squad car, I looked through the window at the crowd of folks gathered around. They'd been so friendly last night. Now their angry stares were tinged with the sting of betrayal.

I knew exactly how they felt.

As the squad car kicked up dust, I watched Maggie and the RV shrink away out of sight, and tried to look on the bright side.

At least now I'd be able to make a phone call.

Chapter Twenty

I knew the drill. I'd only get one call. So, I decided to wait and see how my "interview" with Chief Collins went. If my gut was any indication, I'd be needing an attorney more than I'd be needing Tom.

"Seeing as how you're from out of town, I'd like to give you the benefit of the doubt, Ms. Fremden," Chief Collins said, causing the toothpick between his lips to bob up and down erratically.

I shifted in my chair in the small, sparse room reserved for questioning suspects and witnesses. I wasn't sure if the Chief's soft approach was a "good cop" ploy or just his general nature.

"You see, those folks at Shell Hammock are a tight clan," he continued from his standing position on the opposite side of the wooden table I was seated behind. "I mean, how would *you* feel if a stranger showed up in your little community one day, and next thing you know, your friend gets murdered?"

I swallowed a lump.

"Not good. You said you'd like to give me the benefit of the doubt. Does that mean you think I'm innocent?"

The Chief's lips twisted to one side. "I'd like to think so, but you've got to give me something to work with."

"What do you mean?"

"I'm not one to jump to conclusions so quick as some, but most times, I've found if it smells like a rotten egg, it's a rotten egg. I have to say, the evidence against you doesn't look too good. I mean, I'm not the sharpest man on the force, Ms. Fremden, but you left a trail of clues even my dimwitted son-in-law could follow."

"Clues? *What* clues?"

The Chief pulled the toothpick from his mouth and studied the chewed end.

"Well, there's that pesky blood splatter all over your RV, for one."

"It isn't blood. It's Chef Boyardee."

The Chief nodded slowly and blew out a breath. "All right, then. Supposing it is. How do you explain *this*?"

He slapped my notebook on the table. "Is that your handwriting?"

"Yes."

"And is that your list labeled. 'Ways to get rid of a body?'"

"Uh...yes, but—"

"Kind of a little coincidental, don't you think?"

"Uh...sure. I could see how you could think that. But, here's the thing. I'm taking a class on writing mystery novels. The list is for an assignment."

"An assignment. Uh huh. Who's your teacher?"

"Angela Langsbury."

Chief Collins' face lost a large fraction of its lackadaisical charm.

"Don't get smart with me, Miss Fremden. You think because I live in the country I was born in a watermelon patch?"

"No, sir. I know this must all sound—"

The door squeaked open. Detective Rogers, the cop with the clipboard, entered and handed it to Chief Collins. He proceeded to shoot me a dirty look as the Chief scanned the report.

"Says here the spots in your RV tested negative for blood," Chief Collins said.

"See? I told you. So, are you going to release me?"

Rogers pointed at something on the clipboard. The Chief nodded.

"Oh. All but one," Chief Collins said. "Found a pesky spot of blood on the edge of the table. Human, too." He looked up from the report. "What do you have to say about that?"

"I don't know. I'm not the first person to stay in that place. It could be anybody's."

"Then you won't mind if Detective Rogers here gets a sample of your blood for comparison, right?"

"Uh. No. That's fine."

The words were barely out of my mouth when Rogers grabbed my hand, jabbed my finger, and stuck a pipette on the wound to suck up a sample.

"Ouch!" I cried out. "Are we done now?"

Chief Collins studied the report for a beat before saying, "Not just yet."

He nodded at Rogers and the insolent finger jabber left the room. Chief Collins flipped to the second page of the report.

"There's just a few other little things I want to clear up first."

He eyed on the clipboard. "I have testimony from Elmira Fitch that you accused her of witchcraft and that you put a spell on Wally Walters to make him think he was a toad-frog. Then you lured him into the pool, telling him it was a pond, and drowned him."

My unhinged jaw failed me. "I...I..."

Chief Collins looked up and smiled. "Don't worry about it. We all know Elmira's cornbread ain't quite done in the middle."

I blew out a sigh of relief.

"But her sister Charlene, now she's a bit more reliable—and the busiest busybody this side of the Chattahoochee. Says here she testified that when she returned from the store to deliver the Cheetos and moon pies she'd graciously picked up for you, she overheard you talking on the phone to somebody. You said, quote, 'Things were about to get ugly.' Charlene also said she saw you wiping down your car with a towel that had bloodstains on it."

"That was my 'emergency' towel, and I was talking to...uh...my-self...."

Chief Collins glanced up from the clipboard for a second.

"Uh-huh."

His eyes went back to the report.

"So, last night, during the fish fry, Charlene says that when Woggles went home, you left right after him. I'm quoting here, 'She took off with that new fella without even offering to help clean up. When I walked by a couple hours later, on my way home, bone-tired from cleaning up without her help, I heard somebody holler inside her trailer. Then I heard a thump. I waited around a minute or two, but didn't hear nothing else. So I minded my own business and went home. I never saw Woggles alive after that.'"

"Well...I can explain. You see, that's when I had the accident with the spaghetti sauce. I tripped and knocked it o—"

"You know," Chief Collins cut in, "nothing like this has ever happened at Shell Hammock before. Then you show up and *bam*. Woggles is dead. What do you have to say about that?"

"Uh...I'm renowned for my bad timing?"

Chief Collins chewed his toothpick. "Maybe. But I'm beginning to think there's more to it than that. Take a listen at Slim Johnson's testimony."

He turned the page on the clipboard.

"'It was them cookies. Nobody 'round here bakes cookies. I think she up and poisoned Woggles with them.'"

I choked. "Why would I do that?"

"Good question. Rogers asked Slim the same thing. Here's what he said; 'I don't know. But Charlene said you should check her computer. When she was up in that RV, she seen that woman was writing something about murdering somebody with a snickerdoodle.'"

An elephant stomped on my chest.

Oh, geez! She must have looked at my computer screen. It was open to The Snickerdoodle Murders. *Oh, crap!*

"Ms. Fremden? You still with me?"

"Huh? Yes sir."

"Did those cookies Woggles was eating before he died come from you?"

"Well...uh...I...."

Chief Collins leaned over the table and eyed me like an eagle contemplating a mouse.

"It's not a hard question. Did you make the snickerdoodles found with the deceased Mr. Walters or didn't you?"

I swallowed hard.

"Excuse me, Chief Collins, but I want to speak with my attorney."

"SO LET ME GET THIS straight," J.D. Fellows' voice said over the phone. "You knocked yourself out with a jar of spaghetti sauce after being frightened by what you thought was a demon entity summoned by a shrunken head."

"Correct."

"You went to the trailer park to write a mystery about a guy in a trailer park who dies from eating poisoned snickerdoodles."

"Well, that's not the *only* reason I went, but essentially, yes."

"And a guy there just happened to end up being poisoned by snickerdoodles."

"Uh...that hasn't been totally confirmed yet."

"And you're caught holding a paystub for ten grand."

"I told you, it's Goober's."

"Val, not even *I* would believe that."

"Crap."

"Exactly. You're lucky they're releasing you on your own recognizance. Anything else pertinent I should know?"

"Yeah. Don't trust the Internet. The pictures of that place have got to be thirty years old."

"I said, 'pertinent.'"

"I locked my keys in the trunk of my car. Is it pertinent that I'm stuck here until I can get the trunk open or until Tom finds the spare set and sends it to me?"

"Not really. I'm a lawyer, Val. Not a locksmith."

"I know. But could you call one for me?"

"You don't have a phone?"

"No. I'm calling from the police station. My phone's dead, and I brought the wrong charger."

"Val, that's what we in the business call 'pertinent' information."

"Sorry. What should I do?"

"Take a cab to Walmart. Buy a new charger. While you're there, call a locksmith."

"Okay."

"And don't worry. I know you didn't kill anyone with a snickerdoodle."

"Thanks. And J.D? Do me a favor. Don't tell Laverne. Or Tom. Not yet, anyway. There's no need to get them involved right now."

"Why not?"

"I have my reasons. Oh...and I guess there's one more 'pertinent' thing I should tell you."

"What?"

"The snickerdoodles? They were made by Laverne."

After a long silence, I thought I heard J.D. say, "Aww, shizzlenuts."

Chapter Twenty-One

"Nice digs," the Über driver said as he maneuvered his Ford Fiesta slowly past the falling-down sign for the Hell'ammo. I had to admit, it looked a lot worse in the daylight.

"I'm number thirteen," I said.

"Of course you are." He pulled up in front of the tiny RV and whistled. "Is that your car under the tarp?"

"Yes."

I reached for my push-broom crutch and opened the door. The wiry old driver made no effort to help. He was too busy staring at Maggie.

"Looks like a Ford Falcon," he said.

"Yeah. 1963 Sprint," I grunted as I hoisted myself up out of the seat.

"V-8 engine?"

"Yeah."

I grabbed my Walmart bags, shut the door and limped to the driver's window.

"Dual glass-packs, too. What do I owe you?"

"Eighteen bucks. Does it run?"

"Yeah."

"Why didn't you drive it?"

I blew out a breath and handed him a twenty.

"Locked the keys in the trunk. I'm waiting on a locksmith."

The leathery old man looked me up and down, then eyed the grungy, pink-flecked laundry flapping on the line. He shook his head and grinned, revealing the gap where his four front teeth used to be.

"Tell you what, lady. I'll never complain about my luck again."

"Right," I said sourly. "Keep the change."

He tipped his Redman Chewing Tobacco cap at me and took off down the dirt lane. I watched him go, then hobbled toward the RV.

I had a busted little toe, a broom for a crutch, an empty wallet, a car with no keys, a village of angry rednecks on my back, and a warning from the police to not leave Polk County.

Yep. I was livin' the dream.

On the bright side, I had a new phone charger, a pack of bologna, a jar of pickles and an appointment with a locksmith within the next four hours. At least while I was waiting around, I could try and get some writing done.

When I opened the door to the RV, I realized that was never going to happen. My place had been ransacked.

My computer was gone. Lying on the dinette table in its stead was a set of keys. I scrambled over for a closer look.

"My keys!" I cried.

I couldn't have been happier if it were a box of chocolate-covered cherries from Chocolateers. I grabbed the charger, unwrapped it, stuck it in the wall and let my phone juice up while I put my groceries away. I was nibbling on bologna when a thought finally dawned on me.

Even though I had to stay in *Polk County*, I didn't have to stay *here*.

I snatched up my phone and cancelled the locksmith. Then I dialed the police station.

"Hello? Could I speak with Chief Collins? It's Val Fremden."

I waited on the line for a minute.

"Ms. Fremden? I'm glad you called. I—"

"Listen, Chief Collins, I just wanted to say thanks for finding my keys."

"What?"

"When you came back and re-searched my place. When can I get my computer back?"

"Ms. Fremden, we don't have your computer. And we didn't re-enter your domicile."

"Then who did?"

"I don't know. I was just going to ask you to voluntarily surrender your computer. If this is some kind of ploy to hide evidence...."

"No! It's not! Someone broke in and stole my computer...and returned my car keys. That...that doesn't make any sense!"

"No it doesn't. But I tell you what does. Detective Rogers found a plastic lid in the garbage receptacle outside your unit. It appears someone tried to shred it. But evidently it fits the container found floating next to Wally Walters. Tampering with evidence will only dig you deeper in the hole, Ms. Fremden. And nowadays, it doesn't take but a molecule or two to detect the use of poisons. We're running toxicology tests on everything as we speak."

"But...I'm not lying! Or tampering! I swear!"

"The proof will be in the pudding, Ms. Fremden. Or should I say, in the cookie. Don't leave town."

The line went dead.

Geez Louise! Was I being set up by the folks at the Hell'ammo?

I marched to the freezer. It was gin-and-tonic time somewhere. I flung open the door and instantly forgot all about the Tanqueray.

Propped up against the bag of ice, a hideous little monster grinned at me with sharp, broken-shell teeth.

The shrunken head was back. Only this time, the message accompanying it read:

Get Out Now.

Chapter Twenty-Two

I had orders to not leave town, but it didn't mean I had to stay in Winky's stupid RV—especially now that there was a voodoo head leering at me from the freezer like a deranged Eskimo!

The freezer door nearly came off its hinges as I slammed it shut. I shuffled to the bedroom like a hobbled crab chasing high tide. My suitcase lay open on the bed. It had been rifled through as well. My clothes had been flung everywhere.

I snatched my shorts, shirts and underwear from doorknobs, bedposts and lamps and stuffed them back in the case. I grabbed my toothbrush and makeup from the tiny bathroom, threw them on top of the clothes, and fastened the clasps.

On my way past the fridge, I grabbed the bologna and pickles, shoved them in the Walmart bag and headed for the door. My poor gin would have to deal with Nanook of the Frigidaire on its own. I wasn't opening that freezer door again for anything!

I cracked the RV door open just enough to drop my suitcase outside. Maggie's keys were still lying on the dinette table next to my purse. I hobbled over, got a good grip on my crutch, slung my purse over my left shoulder, and grabbed the keys.

I am soooo outta here!

When I flung open the RV door, I discovered a snag in my hasty getaway scheme. I'd forgotten about Maggie.

She was covered in a silver tarp like an un-popped pan of Jiffy Pop.

Crap!

I set my purse and shopping bag on the steps and limped over to her. My kneecaps cracked as I squatted down and peeled the duct tape off of her left, front side panel. When I struggled back to standing, Stumpy was on the other side of Maggie, staring at me.

"Going somewhere?" he asked in a way that made me think he had other ideas on the matter.

"I uh...."

"Chief tol' me you wasn't supposed to leave."

"He meant Polk County, not Shell Hammock."

I sized up Stumpy. Given his age and watermelon belly, I might could outrun him. I shifted on my crutch and remembered *I was using a crutch.* There went that option.

"Look, Stumpy, I'm sorry about Woggles."

"Sorry you killed him?" His tone sounded more hurt than angry.

"No! I mean, I'm sorry, yes. But not that I killed him...I mean...because *I didn't kill him!*"

Judging by his expression, my eloquent testimony had yet to convince Stumpy of my innocence.

"Who did, then?" he asked, his voice marked with pain and a touch of sarcasm.

I thought about the food at last night's fish fry. I knew my expired Cheeto casserole hadn't killed Woggles, or nobody would be left alive.

"I dunno. Maybe the mayo on those pears last night did Woggles in. It looked like it had gone off to me."

I inched my way to the left rear tire and squatted again. My knees cracked like a walnut in a vice grip.

"I done et five a them thangs myself," Stumpy argued as he came around and met me at the back of the car. "*I'm* still standin.'"

I tugged on the sticky duct tape plastered across the left rear side panel.

"Well, everybody has different tolerances for things."

"How do you know that?"

I looked up at Stumpy. Given his dirty overalls, bare feet and glint in his eye, it wouldn't be long before he was toting a torch and a pitchfork. I hauled myself to standing.

"Listen, Stumpy. I didn't hurt Woggles. Why would I? He seemed like a nice fella. I'm sorry he's gone."

"So why you tryin' to leave in such a hurry?"

"Because I think whoever killed Woggles might be after *me*, too. I found a voodoo head and a nasty note on my door last night."

Stumpy's furrowed brow went slack.

"What're you talkin' about?"

"I got another one today. Inside my freezer. Go look for yourself."

I let Stumpy inside the RV. He came back and stood in the doorframe, the shrunken head in one hand, the bottle of Tanqueray in the other.

"You should be more worried about *this*," he said, and shook the gin bottle at me. "This here ain't no voodoo head. It's...speak of the devil."

"That's what I'm talking about," I said.

But Stumpy wasn't looking at me. I turned to follow his gaze. Poised on the dirt road was Charlene in her shopper chopper. Elmira was riding shotgun again in the basket up front.

"Why you ungrateful hooligan!" Elmira screeched. She whirled her coonskin purse in the air over her head like a shepherd getting ready to let loose with a rock sling.

"Hold up!" Stumpy said. "Why you two got it in for this woman?"

"She called my sister a witch!" Charlene bellowed.

"No I didn't!" I argued.

"Sure did," Charlene countered angrily. "When we was walkin' by her house. I told you Elmira was a crafter. You said it was witchcraft!"

"I only asked—"

"I done give her one a my nicest trinkets," Elmira sneered. "What's she do with it? Throwed it in the yard!"

"What?" I gasped. "I didn't!"

"I seen it yesterday!" Elmira's eyes scanned the ground. "Back up, Charlene. It's gotta be right around here somewheres."

"Wait a minute," I said. "You mean that *shrunken head?* With the note that said, 'Stay Away?' You don't think *that's* witchcraft?"

Stumpy walked to the middle of the space between me and the other women. He held up his short-fingered hands like a referee.

"Now, hold on, ladies. One at a time."

He held up the shrunken head he'd taken from my freezer. The Tanqueray bottle was gone. I didn't notice where it went to.

"Elmira Fitch, what you got to say for yourself?"

"I ain't no witch!" Elmira spat. "That there what she's callin' a voodoo head is a room freshener. You know that, Stumpy Whitehead! It was a welcome gift."

"Then why did the note tell me to 'Stay Away?'" I argued.

"That ain't right. I wrote 'Stay *Awhile*. Or at least, I meant to."

"Oh," I conceded. "The note got wet. It was all smeared.... But wait a minute! Why'd you break into my RV and put it back in my freezer? With a note telling me to 'Get out now!'"

Elmira's face scrunched into a red ball. "I did no sucha thang!"

"Then who did?" a man's voiced boomed out from the bushes. Monster-sized Slim stepped out and joined ranks with Stumpy.

Geez. Now it was four against one.

"What did you do to get that ten thousand dollars?" Slim asked.

"Yeah," Charlene sneered. "Sounds like hit-man money to me."

I took a step back. "It wasn't...that check...it doesn't belong to me."

"Then why was you throwing money around?" Charlene asked, her face pinched into one glaring, three-inch circle.

"You give Woggles a fiver for nothin'. Tried to bribe me, too."

I smiled weakly at Stumpy. He didn't return it.

"Why wouldn't you let Woggles see what was in yore trunk?" Charlene asked.

Stumpy's head cocked to one side. "What'd you need with all that ice?"

"You got a body in that there trunk?" Slim asked.

"That's it!" Charlene cried. "Woggles must a seen the body. So you had to get rid a him!"

I could feel my body shrivel. I backed up. "No. This is all a big misunderstanding...."

"Then why was all your clothes and what-not covered in blood?" Elmira asked.

"*She's* the witch," Charlene said. "She come to the door yesterday totin' a broom. And look at her now. She's still got one!"

Slim snatched my crutch away with his bear-sized paw. In one easy motion, he ripped off the towel duct-taped over the bristles, revealing it was, indeed, a broom.

"I...I didn't kill Woggles!" I screeched.

I took a step toward the RV. But without my crutch, pain shot through my smashed toe, sending me reeling forward. I collapsed in a heap beside Maggie, closed my eyes, and awaited my fate.

I was doomed.

"I THINK IT'S TIME FOR you to go."

I cracked open an eye and caught a glint of gold reminiscent of Laverne's lame jumpsuit.

If only.

Both my eyelids flew up.

Could it be Laverne's come to rescue me from this angry mob?

No such luck. The gold belonged to Steve, or, more precisely, Steve's front tooth.

The smarmy guy feigned a smile from beneath his ball cap. For whose benefit, I wasn't sure. He held out his hand. I took it. He hoisted me to my feet. I noticed his blue t-shirt. It read, *This Never Happened*.

"Party's over," Steve said to the Hell'ammo clan.

"Says who?" Slim asked.

"Yeah," Stumpy joined in. "On whose authority? *Yours?*"

"As a matter of fact, *yes*," Steve said curtly.

He reached in his back pocket.

"I'm on special assignment for Chief Earl Collins. VJU. Vigilante Justice Unit."

Steve flashed his badge and tucked it back in his pocket while the Hell'ammo crowd huddled together and mumbled amongst themselves. They seemed to be taking some kind of vote.

"What you gonna do with her?" Stumpy asked, looking up from the huddle.

"Chief Collins wants me to bring her in for another round of questioning," Steve said. "Now I suggest you all go back to your own business. And don't follow us or you'll be next."

That last bit made more than a couple of eyes widen.

Steve picked up my purse, handed it to me and said, "Hold out your hands."

I did as instructed.

Steve whipped out a pair of handcuffs and clapped them on my wrists. His fingers dug into my upper arm, and he tugged me toward the dirt road.

Relief wasn't a word I'd have used to describe how I felt as we made our way past the suspicious stares of Slim, Stumpy, Elmira and Charlene. But I figured my odds had to be better at the police station than against an angry horde.

Steve led me down the dirt road in silence. Once we rounded a curve out of sight from the others, Steve stopped and let go of my arm.

"I need to check something," he said. "Wait here."

He took a step behind me. The familiar sound of duct tape ripping off a roll sounded. I turned to face him, but before I could speak, Steve slapped a strip of tape over my mouth.

The last thing I saw before the paper sack went over my head was the glint of Steve's gold tooth below his smarmy moustache, and the sound of his voice saying,

"Do exactly what I say and you just might make it out of this alive."

Chapter Twenty-Three

I couldn't see a thing. Had I been saved by Steve...or kidnapped by a serial killer?

The fact that I was now lying on a bed in a moving vehicle didn't seem to favor the former. What kind of police agent had a bed in his van...or truck...or whatever this was?

Blinded by the paper sack over my head, my other senses heightened. My nostrils detected an odor like a pile of dead rats. I could hear music coming from somewhere...most likely the front of the vehicle.

Roger Miller crooning *King of the Road*.

Steve began singing along. The torture had begun.

I tried to get up, but my captor had tied my ankles together after shoving me on the bed. I squirmed around on the mattress like a grub for a while, then gave up.

But my struggling hadn't been totally in vain. Something new appeared in my range of vision. A dim, grey light emanated from around my chin. The bag had moved upward.

Steve hadn't fastened the bag around my neck!

I wriggled down the bed until the paper bag no longer covered my eyes.

In the thick, grey light, I could see I was in an RV. Lumpy, rank-smelling garbage bags hung on the walls. I made out a woman's floppy hat on a shelf. I squinted into the dark and immediately wished I hadn't. Sticking out of the bag closest to me was a ghostly human hand.

The amputated stump's fingers reached outward, frozen by rigor mortis.

Holy mother of Elvis!

The bags swaying on the walls around me were stuffed with the body parts of Steve's other victims!

Something touched my leg. I jerked away as if I'd been hacked with a machete.

I tried to scream bloody murder, but the duct tape over my mouth thwarted my efforts to a desperate mewing. I forced my left eye open and craned my neck to get a look at my leg. To my relief, it was still intact. So was my purse. It was on the bed next to my shin, toppled over on its side.

I almost kicked it off the bed for scaring the crap out of me. But then a thought pierced through my scrambled wits.

That purse might be my only hope.

If I could get to it, maybe there was something inside my handbag that could save me. I folded myself like a pocketknife and reached my cuffed hands toward the handle. Suddenly, the vehicle swerved and lurched to a stop.

The music stopped...

...the engine cut off...

...and footsteps headed my way.

Chapter Twenty-Four

"I see you've been a naughty girl," Steve's voice hissed playfully as he stepped into the tiny room where I lay trussed up on the bed like an injured deer.

"Mmm mmm," I muffled through the duct tape, and shook my head softly in a plea for mercy.

"You really shouldn't have taken that bag off. I wanted to surprise you."

Steve leaned over me, his face just inches from mine. I could smell the sour beer on his hot breath.

"Don't scream," he whispered, then ripped the duct tape from my mouth in one quick, merciless yank.

I hadn't felt pain like that since that one time I'd tried to wax my legs.

"Yowww!" I bellowed.

Steve put his hand over my mouth. "Take it easy."

"Who are you?" I mumbled through his fingers and my glue-sticky lips. "Where are we? What do you want with me?"

"Hold on," Steve laughed cruelly. "Give me a minute."

I struggled to sitting. "And let you murder me out here in the woods?"

Steve laughed again. He reached for something in his shirt pocket. As he leaned over me, with my cuffed hands I grabbed the handle on my purse and walloped him across the face with my hillbilly hacky sack.

He fell on top of me like a bag of doorknobs, knocked out cold.

Adrenalin throbbed in my eardrums. I heaved Steve's limp body aside and plucked feverishly at the fabric binding my ankles. Finally, I felt it give way.

As I inched off the bed, Steve moaned.

Panic shot through me.

Before I knew what was happening, my hands snatched up my purse, raised it in the air, and clobbered Steve once more hard on the noggin. I scooted off the bed and scrambled toward the front of the RV, my toe aching like a sore tooth.

I flung the door wide open, hoping I could find a lone motorist or a homesteader in the woods who I could flag down for help.

I didn't have to look far.

The sickly yellow light of a lamppost revealed that the RV was sitting in the back forty of a Walmart parking lot.

I stood there in the doorway, open mouthed. I was barefoot. In handcuffs. And wearing a paper bag on my head like a makeshift chef's hat.

You *know* you're in trouble when the *people of Walmart* look at you funny.

I SNATCHED THE PAPER bag from my head. I needed to get out of these cuffs.

Calling the police for help seemed like a non-starter. Besides, my phone was dead. I'd only had a couple of minutes to charge it before I got spooked by the lovely parting gift Elmira had left inside my freezer.

Then a thought hit me like a fist in the gut.

As horrifying as it was, my only option at the moment was to go back inside the RV...and retrieve the cuff key from Steve.

I sucked in a Valliant Stranger breath and turned around. As I crept back inside, I left the RV's door open. That way, any Walmart shoppers loitering nearby could hear me scream....

I SEARCHED THE CAB first. A jumble of keys were hanging in the ignition. I yanked them out and sorted through them. Thanks to Tom, I knew what a handcuff key looked like. Unfortunately, the bundle rattling through my shaking fingers didn't contain one.

I dropped the keys into my purse for safekeeping. I wasn't going to let this murderer get away with...you know...*murder.*

A knot twisted in my gut.

If the keys weren't here, that meant....

Crap on a cracked-up cracker.

My gut did a backflip. I shuffled around and stared toward the dark hallway leading to the bedroom. I straightened my shoulders, grit my teeth, and hobbled toward the psycho slaughterer's hideous black lair.

Every hair on my body stood at attention. My mind screamed one continuous, wailing, *Nooooooo!*

IN THE DIM LIGHT, STEVE looked like a gray mannequin. He appeared to still be unconscious, sprawled out on his back in the bed. I leaned over him and patted down his shirt pocket.

Nothing.

I grimaced and reached my cuffed hands into his right pants pocket. I felt something...but it wasn't a key.

Ugh!

I jerked my hands away. Steve groaned.

Lord help me! I need to get those keys before he comes to!

I couldn't see crap. So, I fumbled on the wall for a light switch and flipped it on.

In the blinding light, Steve snorted and rolled onto his side. As he did so, his ball cap and wig remained where they were, like hacked off body parts.

Steve had been wearing a disguise!

It figures! The dirtbag was bald! And his head was....

I stared at Steve's face. My mind's eye filled in his smarmy, pencil-thin moustache until it was as thick as a wooly, brown caterpillar.

Oh my word!

Steve wasn't Steve. Steve was Goober.

I was so shocked I could have beaten Goober senseless.

But I'd already done that.

Chapter Twenty-Five

I laid a cool washrag on Goober's bumpy forehead and looked around the room. Everything was so familiar now.

I could feel my face redden at my own wild imaginings. The garbage bags hanging on the walls...they didn't hold dead bodies, but Cold Cuts' disguises.

I was inside Glad's old RV, not a murder mobile.

The source of the dead-rat smell was as yet to be determined. Perhaps Goober had returned to his old pet-cremation job. Given the other options for the foul odor, I actually hoped that was the case.

Goober groaned. I wiped his brow.

"Are you all right?" I asked, and shook his shoulder gently.

He cracked open a dizzy eye. It focused on me. Goober recoiled like a Mossberg shotgun.

"Stop," he grunted. He kicked his legs feebly like an overturned tortoise and scooted a foot away from me on the bed. "It's me. Goober," he muttered. "Don't—"

I grimaced with guilt. "I know, Goober! I didn't know! I mean, I know *now*. What the heck are you doing here? Were you trying to *murderize* me?"

"What?" Goober grunted. "No. Whatever gave you *that* idea?"

I glanced at the mannequin hand sticking out of a garbage bag, then at my cuffed hands, then at the twin knots growing out of Goober's forehead like devil's horns.

"Gee, Goober, I dunno."

"WERE THE HANDCUFFS and duct tape really necessary?" I asked, and rubbed my freed wrists.

"I didn't have time to explain," Goober said.

He was sitting across from me in the RV's dinette booth nursing his lumps and a beer.

"I knew you'd have to hear every gory detail before you'd go with me."

"That's not true," I sulked, knowing it darn well was.

"Come on, Val. There was no time for Q and A. The natives were getting mighty restless, in case you hadn't noticed."

I conceded with a sneer. "So, where'd you get the badge?"

Goober reached in his back pocket. "You mean this thing?"

He flashed a Donut VIP badge just like the one Winky had given me.

I shook my head and snorted out a laugh.

Goober shot me a crooked grin. His smarmy moustache, combined with the light reflecting off the twin knots on his forehead, made him the spitting image of what I thought a psycho killer should look like.

"I had to rescue you Val, before you succumbed to the dark side."

"Before *I*...? What in blue blazes are you talking about?"

"See? You're already starting to sound like a hillbilly. That twang in your voice? Then that comment you made to Stumpy...that the trailer park *felt like home?* Really, Val. You were one step away from playing a tune on a moonshine jug."

"I was not! And anyway, what were *you* doing there? Did Tom send you to spy on me?"

"Naw."

Goober inspected one of his horn-lumps with his fingertips as he spoke.

"Tom called me and said you needed your spare keys. He'd tried to get back with you, but you never answered. He got worried when he couldn't reach you, and called me. I've recently become a free agent, in case you haven't heard. I volunteered to drop the keys by and make sure you were all right."

"So you *were* spying on me."

"If that's the way you want to look at it. But honestly, I've got better things to do with my life."

I sneered. "Like what?"

"Like rescue you from a pack of wild hillbillies. You're welcome, by the way."

I scrunched my face together until I could spit out an apology.

"Thanks. Sorry I beaned you over the head, but I thought you were about to dismember me."

"You should know me by now. I'm not that ambitious."

I smirked. "What's that thing hanging on your window, there?"

I pointed to a wire clothes hanger hooked over the curtain rod. It had been bent into a lopsided circle. Stretched across it like a Mercedes logo was a pair of women's pink, thong underwear. Below them, tied to the bottom of the hanger with fishing line, hung two empty beer cans and a tin of Skoal chewing tobacco.

"Don't tell me you've never seen one of those before."

"No. Is it some kind of voodoo thing? You know, like the shrunken heads?"

Goober laughed. "Nope. That, my dear, is what they call a 'redneck dreamcatcher.'"

I laughed despite my disgust. "And why do *you* have one?"

"Eh. It's part of my disguise. You'd be surprised how much street cred it gives me with the locals."

I sneered at the crude contraption. "I can only imagine."

I put my elbows on the table and rested my head in my hands. "I guess you know, they all think I murdered Woggles."

"Yeah."

"What do *you* think happened to him?"

"I couldn't say at the moment, Val. But as you know, I always think better with a belly full of tacos."

Chapter Twenty-Six

A crispy corn tortilla met its fate beneath a moustache that looked as if it had crawled out from under a damp rock. As Goober crunched down on the taco, a spray of salsa shot out and splatted onto the left boob area of my shirt, beating me to the punch.

I dabbed at it with a paper napkin. "So what are you doing in Glad's...I mean *Cold Cuts'* RV?"

"As they say, life is an ever-evolving process," Goober waxed philosophically.

"Jorge threw you out?"

Goober shrugged. "More like Sherryl. Though I really can't blame either of them. Love birds tend to prefer an empty nest."

"One without a Cuckoo in it," I said, and laughed at my own joke. "So, you flew the coop, eh?"

Goober stared at me. "You done with the bad bird puns?"

I sighed defeat. "Yeah."

"With my options recently opening up, I decided to give the RV lifestyle a try. Cold Cuts offered me hers on a trial basis. She doesn't get much use out of it now that she's with Bill down at the resort. Mind if I order another taco?"

I shrugged. "Why should I care?"

"Well, the tab's on you. I'm kind 'a short on cash at the moment."

"Wait a minute. What about that check you just got for ten grand?"

Goober choked on his taco. "What check?"

I fished in my purse and pulled out the greasy check stub. "*This* one."

"What the...how did...that's not mine."

"Right." I pulled out the other paystub. "It sure wasn't from working at Griffith & Maas."

Goober's lips followed the shift of his eyes to the left. "You got that right."

"So where'd you get that kind of money, Goober? Are you like...a *hitman* or something?"

"*Really*, Val?"

I crinkled my nose. "Witness protection program?"

Goober sighed and shook his head. "No."

"What, then?"

"Listen, if I tell you, then I'll have to—"

"Kill me, right?"

"No." Goober's eyes turned serious, then bore into mine. "I'll have to disappear."

GOOBER AND I AGREED to put a pin in his check stub for the moment and concentrate on the looming problem at hand. Who'd killed Woggles?

We strolled back across the lamp-lit parking lot to the RV, after a quick stop in Walmart for a six-pack and a plastic bag of popcorn the size and shape of the cashier's thigh who rang us up.

"I have a confession to make," I said.

"Don't tell me. You actually *did* kill that poor, cross-eyed old redneck," Goober joked.

"Ha ha. *No*. But Goober..." I looked around and lowered my voice. "...maybe *Laverne* did. Think about it. I know Woggles ate at least one bite from a cookie she baked."

"Oh, crap."

"Exactly. What's the going rate for unintentional homicide?"

Goober looked taken aback.

"How should *I* know? Geez. But one bite. That's not enough to...well...no. We *are* talking about Laverne's cooking here."

I nodded solemnly. "The police are still waiting on the toxicology report."

"Did you tell Chief Collins about Laverne?"

"No. That's when I pled the Fifth and called J.D. *He* knows."

"You talked to J.D.? What did he say about this whole...*situation?*"

I winced. "That I was lucky not to be hanging from a rope already."

Goober whistled. "That bad, huh? Okay. Let's pin Laverne up there with me for now. Who else could have done-in Woggles?"

"I couldn't say. In the South, a mean streak can run deep and silent. And then one day—*bam!*"

Goober sidestepped away from me. "Thanks for the warning."

"Really?"

"Didn't you notice the puddle?" he joked. "As you were saying."

"My gut tells me Elmira had something to do with it. She's creepy...and craftier than you might think. She's the one who made that shrunken head and wrote those threatening notes. First, 'Stay Away,' which she claims was 'Stay Awhile,' but then the second one said 'Get out now.' She couldn't so easily explain *that one* away."

I handed Goober back his keys. He fiddled with the lock until he opened the RV door. As he climbed the steps, he turned and said, "Elmira couldn't explain that second note because she didn't write it."

"Who did?" I asked as I followed him inside the Minnie Winnie.

"*I* did."

"What? *You?*"

"Yeah. I was the one who broke into your lovely tin-can cottage by the sea."

"Why?"

I plopped onto the dinette bench. My toe was aching. I cracked open a beer. Goober twisted a can from the plastic ring and put the rest in the tiny fridge.

"Well, originally I was just going to leave the keys to Maggie for you to find, as if you'd lost them. I used the spare keys to retrieve the set you locked in the trunk. Smooth move, by the way."

Goober winked and shot me with a finger gun. I shot him back with a nasty sneer as he slid into the bench across the table from me.

"Anyway, I was committing the B&E when I heard someone coming, so I hid in the bushes. I overheard Charlene talking to Slim about how you were writing a story about killing someone with poison snickerdoodles. I mean really, Val. That's crazy. Even for *you*."

"It was a class assignment!"

I ripped into the bag of popcorn and grabbed a handful. Goober picked up a kernel and popped it into his mouth.

"Whatever. Anyway, I figured it would definitely *not* be in your best interest for your computer to fall into the wrong hands, so I—"

"*You* have my computer?!"

Goober shrugged. "Yeah."

I felt ten pounds lighter. "Oh! I could kiss you! I thought my stories were lost forever!"

Goober's left eyebrow shot up. "Really? *That's* what you were worried about?"

"Oh. Well, *no*. I mean...it isn't *all* I was worried about. You have no idea how hard it is to write a book!"

"Well, let's just hope that when you're done with it, they don't throw it at you."

"Har har. Very funny."

"Okay. Assuming Laverne and Elmira didn't do it, who else could have killed Woggles?"

"Bigfoot?" I asked.

"That does it. I'm going to bed." Goober took a slug of beer and rubbed the sizable twin lumps swelling above his eyebrows. "For some reason, I have a headache."

I grimaced with guilt and sympathy. "Sorry again."

Goober stood up. I grabbed his hand. "Goober, does Tom know everything?"

"Pretty much. You want to use my phone to call him?"

"No. Thanks. I'll charge mine and call him in the morning."

SOUTHERN GUILT MADE me insist that Goober take the bed. I kept an eye on him from a folding chair in the hallway. I was afraid I might have given him a concussion, so I wanted to make sure he kept on breathing through the night.

When he started snoring like an asthmatic goat, I remembered I'd forgotten to ask him where he'd stashed my computer.

Dang it!

I got up and quietly rummaged through the old Minnie Winnie from top to bottom. Goober must have hidden my laptop well, in case the cops decided to search for it.

I went back to my chair by the bedroom door and watched him breathe for a few minutes. There was a lot I didn't know about Goober. But one thing was for sure. He was a good friend. He had had my back.

Bone-tired, I closed my eyes and nodded off in the chair....

Chef Boyardee was in a red speedo, swimming around in a pool of marshmallow fluff. He spied me sitting on the pool steps. His chef's hat bobbed up and down as his arms wind-milled through the water toward me like an electric beater. He stopped in front of me, shook his smiling head, and stomped on my little toe.

I awoke in a start. My toe was throbbing, and an idea was spinning in my head.

The space above the stove in Winky's RV...where I'd found the jars. I hadn't looked for the laptop there!

I drug the folding chair into the kitchen and found a flashlight under the sink. I climbed up on the chair, opened the cabinet, and peered inside.

Chef Boyardee's instincts had been right. But what the flashlight illuminated wasn't my computer. It was something way, way more precious than that.

Chapter Twenty-Seven

M*y Dearest, Most Beloved Child,*
Wherever you are, whatever name you've been given, to me you will always be my beautiful dragonfly. My precious angel on the wing.

I never got to see you walk, or smile with pearly little teeth, but I've pictured you in my mind a million times.

I know it would take a true miracle of God for this letter to ever reach you. But miracles have been known to happen. I held one in my arms once, long ago.

Even so, sometimes I can scarcely believe you really do exist out there, somewhere. It's those times I look at your photograph, and remember the truth. I truly was blessed.

Believe me when I tell you that I never wanted to let you go, my sweet angel. But I had to. For your sake.

I hope one day you'll understand.

With all the love a mother can have for her beautiful daughter,

Your mom,

Gladys

A tear splashed down heavy on the small photo in my hand. No bigger than a postage stamp, the faded, black-and-white memory had been accompanied by miracle in the form of a fragile, yellowed note.

God had granted Glad's wish. Her daughter had found her letter. And she understood.

In a way, God had granted my wish, too. I'd never known how I'd come to be lying on the side of the road...to be found by my adoptive father Justas. Had I been abandoned by Glad? Thrown out by her horrible husband Bobby? Stolen and ditched by one of Tony's disapproving father's minions?

Now I knew. I'd been loved. So much so that Glad had given me up to *protect* me. To give me a chance at a better life.

In the dim gray of night, the walls of her old RV wrapped around me like a womb. I stared at the miniscule photo of a woman holding a tiny baby in her arms, and let my heart break open and the tears flow.

Chapter Twenty-Eight

I snorted myself awake. I was hunched over on the dinette bench, my head resting on my purse on the table. I lifted my noggin. The muscles in my neck protested so strongly I groaned.

I rolled my head to one side and rubbed my neck. Sometime during the night, I'd decided that my purse would make an excellent pillow. It was lying sideways on the table in front of me, the impression of my face pressed into it, its contents spilled out like the entrails of a possum caught under the wheels of a Ford F-150.

The devil was at the stove making coffee. I was ready to sell my soul to him for a cup.

"Mornin', sleeping beauty," Goober teased as he rubbed one of the red lumps on his forehead. "What'cha got there?"

I looked down at the letter in my hand. I inhaled sharply and pressed it to my chest. "It's...a...love letter."

"From Tom?"

"Uh...no."

"And I thought *I* had secrets."

Goober poured coffee into two mugs. "You take it black?"

"With milk."

"Well, unless you know a friendly cow nearby, I'm afraid this is it."

"I'll take it," I said, and grabbed the mug he offered.

"Speaking of secrets, Goober, let's get back to yours. What's up with the ten grand? And what did you mean when you said you'd have to disappear if you told me?"

"Don't ask."

Goober sighed and took a sip of coffee.

"I just did. Come on."

"Geez! Are you always this feisty in the morning?"

"You haven't begun to *see* my feisty."

"Good grief. How does Tom do it?"

Goober picked up an envelope from the table and waved it at me.

"If you must know, I have to disappear because the AARP found me."

"Yeah, right. Come on, Goober. They find *everybody*."

"Exactly."

Goober tossed the AARP envelope back on the table. I set my mug down on it like a coaster.

"I'm serious, Goober."

"So am I. Val, if I tell you, I'll have to leave all this behind."

Goober swept his free hand in the air around the kitchen, like a merchant displaying his fine wares. I wasn't buying it.

"It's just a broken down, old RV," I muttered.

Goober dropped his hand and shrugged. "It means a lot more than that to me."

Images began to flash in my mind like a series of photographs. The first was of crazy Glad, busy plastering the Minnie Winnie's walls with decals of dragonflies. Next came Cold Cuts and me donning disguises to go crash someone's bad date. Silly stakeouts with the guys. And the nights I'd spent in here alone, talking things out with the mother I wished I'd had more time to get to know.

I looked up at Goober. "I guess I kind of get that."

He sighed and slid into the booth opposite me.

"So, have you called Tom yet?"

"No."

"You're in up to your eyeballs, Val. What are you waiting for?"

"I can't have some man running to my rescue every time I'm in trouble, Goober. I need to stand on my own."

"No you don't."

"Who are you to talk, Marlboro mystery man?"

Goober sneered, making him look like a devil in a wife-beater t-shirt.

"Like I said, I'm not saying. But I'll tell you *this*. Being on your own isn't all it's cracked up to be. There's no sin in needing someone, Val."

I scowled. "I guess it wouldn't hurt to get Tom's professional advice."

Goober grinned. "There you go."

"Do me a favor, would you?"

"What?"

"Lose the gold tooth?"

Goober laughed and touched his mouth. "I'll be in the bathroom if you need me."

He ambled off as I dialed Tom's number.

"Hey, Tom."

"Val! You okay?"

"Yeah, I'm all right."

"Where are you?"

"With Goober in the RV."

"Good. I wish I could be there instead."

"Me, too. But it's okay. I'm doing fine. J.D. said they don't have enough evidence to hold me."

Tom's voice changed an octave. "Hold you? For what?"

"I...I thought Goober told you."

"Told me what?"

Oh, crap!

"I kind of got...accused of murder."

"What?" Tom screeched. "Not again!"

"It's okay. I didn't do it."

"Val! I know that. But I mean...ugh! What happened?"

"An old man at Shell Hammock died. And I just happened to be writing a story about an old man getting murdered in a trailer park..."

"Why on Earth?"

"It was a class assignment!"

"Oh, geez, Val."

"Tom, the cops want my computer. Do you think I should give it to them?"

"Absolutely. Hand it over and cooperate. It's the only way. If they apprehend you trying to flee with it, you're toast."

"Okay. And Tom?"

"Yeah?"

"I—"

The deafening honk of a bullhorn sounded outside. Over a megaphone, a voice demanded, "Come out with your hands up."

"Oh crap. Tom, I gotta go."

I PEEKED OUT THE RV window. Unless it was "Free Donuts for Cops Day" at Walmart, every cop car in Polk County was hot on our trail. We were surrounded like a wagon train, and Chief Collins was leading the roundup.

I open the RV door and stood in the doorframe with my hands up. Chief Collins peeked his jowly face from around the open door of a squad car.

"Step out, Fremden. Anybody else in there?"

"Yes. My friend Goo...uh...Gerald."

"Tell him to come on out, too. Hands in the air."

"I can't. He's kind of...*indisposed*."

"Disposed! Did you kill him, too?"

"No! He's in the bathroom!"

An officer approached and patted me down.

"She's clean."

"Go get the other one," Chief Collins said as he stepped from behind the car door.

The officer pulled his revolver, crept up the stairs, and disappeared inside the RV.

Chief Collins took his time approaching me. Probably so I could get a good look at his smug face. He hitched a thumb in his belt loop and rocked onto his tiptoes and back.

"Got word you were trying to flee the area, Fremden. Not smart."

"Chief Collins, if I'd been trying to flee, do you really think I'd have parked at Walmart? Or stayed overnight?" My stomach growled like an angry grizzly. "Or eaten dinner at Tito's Tacos?"

He looked me up and down.

"I've seen stupider moves by people on the lam."

"I'm not on the lam, sir. I just...well...kind of wore out my welcome at the Hell'ammo."

Chief Collins smiled with one side of his mouth.

"Knowing those folks, I guess I can understand that. But what I don't get is why your friend there thought it was okay to impersonate an officer."

I looked back to see Goober being led out of the RV in handcuffs. "He just—"

"If you don't mind, I'd like to hear it from his own lips."

The officer shoved Goober up beside me.

"What's your name, son?" Chief Collins asked him.

"Jonohhovitz."

"Can you spell that?"

"Yes. But it might take a while."

"Sense of humor, huh? Well, you might need that where you're going."

Chief Collins turned to me. "But first, I'm gonna need that computer of yours, Ms. Fremden."

I looked over at Goober.

"I'll get it," he said.

"Follow him in," Chief Collins said to the officer. "If he tries anything funny, punch him in the gut. From the looks of it, knocking him on the head is ineffective."

I bit my lip and held my arms behind my back.

For the second time in less than twenty-four hours, I was being cuffed and hauled away.

Chapter Twenty-Nine

"Says here she's been researching poisons online," Detective Rogers said as he pecked through my computer's browser. "Cyanide, mostly. But took herself a good, long gander at arsenic, too."

"You don't say," Chief Collins said, swiveling in his chair. He leaned his elbows on his desk and looked me over.

"It was a class assignment," I offered weakly.

"Let me guess. From Angela Lansbury, right?"

I grimaced. "*Langs*bury."

"Uh-huh."

He turned back to Rogers, who was still pecking away at my laptop.

"When we getting those toxicology reports back?"

"Any time now, Chief."

Chief Collins shook a toothpick out of a silver container on his desk.

"Well, Ms. Fremden, I don't have to tell you that this isn't looking too good for you. Why don't you just save us all some trouble and confess."

"To what? I didn't kill Woggles!"

He bit down on the toothpick and grinned. "Then why was his blood found in your RV?"

"Uh, Chief," Rogers said, looking up from my computer. "The blood type didn't match Woggles. It matched *her*, though."

"Hmmm."

Chief Collins made a steeple with his fingers.

"Pray tell, why were you bleeding, Ms. Fremden? Injure yourself struggling with Woggles?"

"Wha—?"

Chief Collins leaned in closer.

"What's the matter? Did Mr. Wallace refuse to eat your poisonous cookies...so you shoved them down his throat?"

"No! That's not what happened!"

"Then enlighten me, Ms. Fremden. How'd your blood come to be on that table?"

"I...I stuck my finger on something."

"What?"

I bit my lip. "Hand me my purse and I'll show you."

Chief Collins eyed me sideways as he reached for my handbag.

"Don't try any monkey business."

He hesitated a moment, then handed me my pocketbook. I pulled out my silver badge.

"Impersonating an officer," he said dryly. "Seems to be a rash of that going on lately."

"No sir. It's a Donut VIP badge." I held it up for his inspection. "See?"

"So, you think law enforcement's nothing but a joke, do you?"

"No! That's not what I meant at all!"

The Chief's eyes shifted from hard to frosty.

"Well, while we're waiting on the coroner's report, I suggest you stay at the Polk Regency."

"Uh...thank you, Chief."

I stood up to leave. "How do I find it?"

"Don't worry. You're already here. Rogers, put her in cell seven."

"My pleasure, sir," Detective Rogers said. He shot me a sneer and took me by the arm.

As he tugged me toward the door, I turned back toward Chief Collins.

"Sir, I really need to talk to you. I have an idea about—"

Chief Collins chewed his toothpick and leaned back in his chair. "Yeah? Well don't we all."

Rogers yanked me out of the office. As he led me down the hall toward the holding cells, I caught a glimpse of Goober walking out the front door, a free man.

"You released *him*, but not *me*?" I asked, bewildered.

"Well now, we can't always get what we want, can we, sweetheart?"

Rogers gave me a push. His lips formed a sarcastic smile, and he slammed the cell door shut between us.

"WAKE UP. YOU GOT A visitor," Detective Rogers barked.

With much effort, I cracked open an eye. I'd passed out on the cot. I could have slept another two days.

"Who? Where?" I mumbled.

I tried to sit up, but gravity felt a lot stronger inside a jail cell.

"Me. Here," a voice said.

A diminutive man in a sharp suit stepped from behind a corner. The sight of him renewed my energy like a gallon of Red Bull.

I sat up and cried, "J.D.!"

Rogers snorted. "Let's hope his bark is bigger than his butt."

J.D. looked up at the detective and smiled.

"Say something like that to me again and I'll be the new owner of every last one of your worldly possessions."

Rogers dried up and blew away like a snot flake in a sandstorm.

J.D. watched him go, then turned to me and said, "I gotta retire."

"SO HOW'S MY CASE LOOKING?" I asked from between the bars in my holding cell.

"Not good," J.D. admitted. "Do you have any new information you want to share with me?"

"I dunno. I know this sounds crazy..."

J.D.'s silver eyebrows ticked upward, but his expression remained as unchanged as a stone. He looked like a man who'd heard it all before, because, mostly thanks to me, he *had*.

"...but I keep thinking about *raccoons*," I said. "Woggles wore a coonskin cap, you know. And I think his belt was made from a possum pelt."

"Woggles? Raccoons? Possums?" J.D. shook his head. "I'm from D.C., Val. The only vile creatures I'm familiar with have elected positions."

A hearty laugh rang out from around the corner. Chief Collins stepped into view.

"Sorry, buddy," J.D. spat. "Freak show's over."

Chief Collins' jovial expression evaporated.

"My apologies, Mister Attorney Man. I already spoke to Detective Rogers about his unfortunate remark. Some folks around here don't have any manners to mind."

"I appreciate that," J.D. countered, "but I would like to exercise my client/attorney privilege now, if you don't mind."

"I don't mind at all," Chief Collins said, and took a step closer. "But earlier today, Ms. Fremden said she wanted to talk to me. I thought maybe the three of us could kill two birds with one stone."

Chief Collins scowled and his ears turned red. "Pardon me. That was an ill-thought out analogy."

J.D. turned and looked me in the eye. "What do you think?"

"He knows more about varmints than you do."

"What's a varmint?" J.D. asked.

Chief Collins grinned. "I believe the little lady just proved her point."

"FUNNY YOU SHOULD MENTION raccoons," Chief Collins said. "Rogers found a dead one in that RV that belongs to your friend Johna.... Johova.... *Gerald*."

"That explains the smell," I said.

"Gerald?" J.D. asked.

"Goober," I explained. "He drove Cold Cuts' RV over here to bring me the spare keys to Maggie."

"Maggie?" Chief Collins asked.

"My car," I said.

"Oh," the Chief replied, and chewed his toothpick.

J.D. cleared his throat. "Now that all that's been cleared up, can we get back to the raccoons?"

"Right."

I leaned back in the comfy chair in the Chief's office and tried to appear as if I had something very, very worthwhile to say. I didn't. All I really had was a nagging suspicion. It wasn't even a full-fledged hunch.

"Woggles really seemed to like raccoons," I began.

"Well, there's no accounting for taste," J.D. said.

I pursed my lips, hoping to increase the strength of my telepathic message to J.D.; *You're not helping.* I directed my next words to Chief Collins.

"Besides his hat, Woggles made Elmira a purse out of a raccoon hide."

"Elmira Fitch."

The Chief said her name as if it tasted bad. He blew out a breath and continued.

"Yes. I believe that she and Mr. Walters were...uh...*close*. I do have some concerns about her. She's one jealous woman. I can see where she might have seen you as a threat."

"But why would she kill *Woggles* if she didn't like *me?*"

Chief Collins looked me in the eye and spoke slowly.

"Not every aimed arrow flies true."

My forehead went slack to match my jaw.

"Oh."

I looked over at J.D. He was on his knees in the chair beside me, busily scribbling into a notebook he'd perched on the armrest like a makeshift desk.

"Detective Rogers searched Woggles place after he died," Chief Collins continued. "His RV was loaded with raccoon pelts. I believe you were trying to make a point about that, Ms. Fremden?"

I swallowed hard, trying to digest my own bull-crap.

"I dunno. Do you think maybe *they*...you know...the *raccoons* could have killed him? You know, like they...you know...ganged up on him while he was in the truck-bed pool? Could they maybe have maybe, you know...drowned him...out of revenge?"

J.D. put his head in his hands.

Chief Collins didn't take it so hard.

"Hmmm," he said, and leaned back in his chair. He chewed on his toothpick enthusiastically as he contemplated my theory.

"I once saw a raccoon drown a hound dog that was chasing him across a river."

He sat back up in his chair. "You could be on to something there, Ms. Fremden. I believe if Woggles had been drinking...I mean, well, I've lived in Florida long enough to know that darn near *anything's* possible."

"Chief Collins," J.D. asked, tapping a pen on his notebook. "Can you tell me how it was possible for Mr. Woggles to capture so many of these raccoon animals?"

Chief Collins leaned back again and squeezed his chin between his thumb and index finger.

"Now *that's* a good question. I don't recall the report saying anything about any traps being found around his place."

By some miracle, my random, bull-crap thoughts formed into a fully-formed cow patty of an idea. I bolted upright in my chair.

"Chief Collins!" I nearly shouted. "That dead raccoon you found in Goob...Gerald's RV. Could we get it tested or autopsied or whatever you do to figure out why an animal died?"

"I suppose so. I think it's still in the dumpster out back. Why?"

"Well, I'm not sure. But maybe whatever killed *it*, might hold a clue about how...or *who*...killed Woggles."

"It's worth a shot," Chief Collins said, and reached for his desk phone. "And I got the perfect detective for the job."

Chapter Thirty

"Thanks for posting my bail," I said to J.D. as my butt sank into the luxurious softness of the white-leather seats in his Mercedes Benz.

"That's what I came here for," he said, and mashed the raised gas pedal designed to accommodate his small frame. "Glad we could work it out."

"I couldn't have done it without you. You're a miracle worker. Take a left out of the parking lot."

J.D. turned the steering wheel and adjusted the rearview mirror. The sunlight caught one of the huge diamonds on his gold watch and laser-beamed me in the retina.

"Actually, you deserve the credit," J.D. said. "Chief Collins was impressed with your cooperation."

"Really?" I said, blinking back the orange dots dancing around in the air. "So he believes me? That I'm innocent, I mean?"

"Well, I wouldn't go that far. It's more like he can't believe anybody could be so dumb as to incriminate themselves as thoroughly as you have."

"What?"

I plastered on my best scowl, but J.D. wasn't paying any attention. He was too busy watching the traffic whizzing by on SR 60.

"Do I turn left or right here?" he asked.

I traded my wasted scowl for a sulking pout.

"Take a right. Does this mean I can go home now?"

"Well, not exactly."

J.D. mashed the gas and took off like Mario Andretti. I gripped the cushy armrest. My fingers sunk into it like it was made of marshmallow fluff.

"Oooh," I cooed.

J.D. eyed me up and down. I stopped squeezing the fancy merchandise.

"As part of your bail agreement, you need to stick around town until the coroner's report comes back. You're not quite off the hook yet, Val. But at least you're no longer the only bait in town. Not where Chief Collins is concerned, anyway."

"Thank goodness for friends in high places."

J.D. gave me another quick study. "I don't know how 'high' either of us are."

"You're both higher than me. I mean, I feel like I should be riding in a cattle trailer behind you. Look at my clothes. I'm probably ruining your leather seats as we speak!"

J.D. looked horrified for a split second, then caught himself. "You don't look that bad."

"Turn here," I said. "J.D., I've been in these shorts and t-shirt for over two days."

J.D.'s lips pursed into a twisted grin. "I thought it was the raccoon."

"You jerk!" I teased, and bopped him on the arm. "Turn in here. Drop me off at the front of the store."

"Okay," J.D. said. "But listen. I'm heading back to civilization. Lay low for the next day or so. Don't do anything stupid, okay?"

"Me? Do something stupid? Not a chance."

J.D. stopped his Mercedes, temporarily blocking the pedestrian cattle-crossing leading up to the entrance to Walmart. I cracked open the passenger door, letting in the oppressive heat. I stuck a foot out onto the half-melted asphalt.

"Thanks again for the ride...and everything."

"So, you'll be all right, on your own?" he asked.

"I'm part redneck, J.D. Who says I'm on my own?"

I grinned and tilted my frizzy-haired head toward the storefront.

J.D. leaned over and peeked out my side window. "What?"

"Look closer."

J.D. pulled off his Gucci sunglasses and strained his eyes toward the Walmart entrance.

To the left of the sliding glass doors, a shabbily dressed old man was dancing for tips. He suddenly stopped, tipped his top hat toward us, and smiled. As he did, a shiny gold tooth glinted in the midday sun.

"Argh!" J.D. groaned. "Don't tell me."

"It's—" I began.

J.D. stuck his fingers in his ears. "If that's Goober, I don't want to know."

"I THOUGHT I TOLD YOU to ditch the gold tooth," I said as Goober picked up his Starbucks tip cup.

He shrugged. "I dunno. It's kind of growing on me."

"Like mold?"

"Look who's talking. Those clothes should be burned at the stake." Goober grinned. "You as hungry as you look?"

"Now that you mention it, I'm starved."

Goober rattled the change in the paper coffee cup.

"Where can a recently cashed up fellow take a girl out around here?"

I peeked in the cup. "Just how cashed up are you?"

Goober poured the change into his hand. "Dang. A dollar thirteen."

I shrugged. "Not bad for a few minutes work."

Goober slid the change into his pocket. "I've been here three hours."

"Oh. Well, with that kind of money, we could split a Yoo Hoo."

"Geez. Don't tell me you're as broke as I am."

"No," I shrugged. "Just kidding. Dinner's on me. It's only fair. You're paying for lodging tonight."

I nodded my head in the direction of the old Minnie Winnie still parked out in the back section of Walmart's blacktop oasis.

"Right. Thanks. Tell you what, Val. You can have the bed tonight."

I took my top-hatted friend by the arm.

"Such a gentleman."

He grinned. "I do my best."

"You up for tacos again?" I asked as we strolled through the crowd spilling out of Walmart.

Goober raised his head high and put a hand on my forearm.

"Always, m' lady."

TITO'S TACOS SMELLED like lard mixed with cumin and desperation. I felt right at home.

"How'd you get released so fast?" I asked Goober as I slid into the greasy booth.

Goober shrugged and took a seat across from me.

"I made a phone call. Pulled a few strings."

"I bet you did. What kind of strings?"

Goober shot me a look.

"I know. I know. You can't tell me. Well, let *me* tell *you* this. The Chief seemed really pissed about you walking out the door."

Goober sighed. "I wasn't put on this Earth to make everybody happy."

"What *were* you put on this Earth to do, Goober? I have a feeling being a *fartist* isn't your only major skill."

"Don't worry about that, Val. Save your worrying for yourself. You're the one who needs it at the moment."

"Why did you have that dead raccoon in the RV?"

"I thought it might come in handy."

"Come in handy? For what? Dinner?"

Goober shrugged.

"Wait a minute. You had your suspicions, too, didn't you?"

"Raccoons don't generally up and die. Not in public, anyway."

"I asked Chief Collins to have it tested."

Goober smiled at me softly. "Then you did good."

A waitress dressed in an embarrassingly cheap-looking, tassel-lined vest and matching red-felt sombrero waddled up to our booth.

"What'll ya have?" she asked, then smacked on a huge wad of pink bubblegum.

"I'll have a pair of your finest tacos, madam, and your cheapest tequila," Goober said. He tipped his top hat for emphasis.

The waitress stopped chomping on her gum.

I smirked and said, "I'll have the same."

I COULD FEEL "THE URPS" coming on as we walked from the restaurant through the parking lot toward the RV.

As we crossed from one line of parked cars to the next, I realized my little toe wasn't aching as much. Instead of looking like a plum stuck to the side of my green flip-flops, it now was masquerading as a red grape.

"Goober, look! My—"

"Shhh!" Goober hissed. He grabbed me by the arm and yanked me behind an enormous, black SUV.

"Ouch!" I cried out. "Watch the merchandise!"

"Sorry. It was an emergency."

"What do you mean?"

"Look for yourself."

My line of sight followed the trajectory of Goober's boney finger all the way to the Minnie Winnie.

Circling it like four well-fed vultures were Stumpy, Slim, Charlene and Elmira.

"Crap! What are we gonna do now?"

"Go back to Tito's and stand out front. I'll infiltrate the crowd."

"Goober, no! Four against one? It's too dangerous!"

"Not really. You forget. They've only seen me as Steve."

"Oh. That's right! Who are you now?"

"Hobo Howard."

I looked him up and down. "Of course you are."

Goober turned to go.

"Wait. You've got to do something about that smarmy moustache. It's a dead giveaway."

"I'm way ahead of you." Goober pulled a small box from his shirt pocket. "I always carry an emergency moustache with me."

My face impersonated a dead trout.

Goober shook his head. "Just walk back over to the taco place. I'll pick you up there."

I'D BARELY PUT MY FOOT on the curb in front of Tito's when I heard tires squeal. I whirled around and saw the Minnie Winnie take a turn on two wheels. It cleared an old lady pushing a shopping cart and then slammed back onto the asphalt. The chassis bounced and lurched and squealed like a mattress at a disreputable motel.

A second later, the RV screeched to a halt at my feet. Goober waved at me from the driver's seat, his moustache at half-mast.

"Get in! Hurry!"

I yanked open the cab door and took a bum dive inside. My feet were still dangling out the door as Goober mashed the gas and sped off.

I scrambled around to right myself in the seat and slammed the door shut.

"Nice entry," Goober said.

"Thanks. I think." I strapped myself into the seatbelt as Goober peeled out of the parking lot.

"Where to now?"

"The Hell'ammo."

"What! Why?"

"You've got to get Maggie back...and your other stuff."

"Yeah, but I don't think *now* is such a good time."

Goober turned and grinned like a wiseacre.

"I wasn't put on this Earth to come up with good ideas. But surprisingly often, I do. Don't you see, Val? Now's the *perfect* time to go. We know where all those folks are, and we've got at least a two-minute lead."

Who was I to argue with a man wearing half a fake moustache?

Chapter Thirty-One

"I don't know about this," I told Goober as the old Minnie Winnie sped east down SR 60 toward the rural RV outpost affectionately known as the Hell'ammo.

"Relax, Val. You think just like a redneck. Believe me, this is *the last* place they'll come looking for us."

"I might be part redneck, Goober, but I'm not stupid."

"On the contrary," he said, and flung his top hat back into the bowels of the RV. "You should be proud of being a redneck."

"Kiss my grits."

Goober laughed, then turned into Professor Peanuthead.

"The term redneck has a rich etymology in the US."

I eyed him suspiciously. "A rich *what?*"

Goober smirked and rolled his eyes.

"*History*, okay? I read somewhere that the whole 'redneck' thing started with a coal miner uprising. The Blair Mountain Battle, if I recall correctly. That's one of the first times working-class folks got tired of their lot and fought back against their employers. The miners wore red bandanas around their necks, hence coining the term 'rednecks.'"

My eyebrows ticked up a notch.

"Huh. So, rednecks were America's first 'power to the people' freedom fighters?"

Goober shrugged. "I don't know about the *first*, but yeah, in a way, that's right."

I settled back into my seat, crossed my arms, and let a warm, satisfying smugness envelope my tired, half-redneck body.

"WE'RE HERE," GOOBER said, startling me awake.

"Nyu-huh?" I grunted.

Geez, how tired did I have to be to doze off in the middle of running for my life?

I looked around. Through the greyish-pink of dusk, I could just make out the overgrown entrance to the Hell'ammo across the paved road.

Goober had backed the RV up into a tangled cover of scrub oaks and palmettoes. Our current covert position afforded a head-on view of the entryway to the redneck lair.

I supposed, logistically, Goober's choice would also aid in making a quick getaway, should one become necessary.

"What's the plan?" I asked, suddenly wide awake.

"You'll go first," he said, and handed me a flashlight. "I'll illuminate the road with the headlights until you drop out of sight. Then use your torch."

"Uh...okay. You're not coming?"

"Only if I spot trouble. I'll honk or something to let you know if anybody comes back."

"Great."

"Look, I'll be right behind you. It's better if we split up, in case one of us gets...caught."

Goober's stomach gurgled like a fountain of mud.

"You need to use the toilet, don't you," I said.

"You know what they say about tacos, Val. They're the 'beer' of food. Tasty going down, but they don't stick around."

I weighed my options. I could stay here, or sneak through the back-woods of Florida alone, unarmed, and in the dark. I chose the woods. The odds of being exposed to something lethal seemed smaller.

"Whatever," I muttered, and slipped out of the RV and into the night.

I'D BARELY MADE IT past the ramshackle sign for the Hell'ammo when Goober killed the headlights. I switched on the flashlight.

Nothing happened.

I panicked and shook the daylights out of it. A feeble, bluish light blinked on and illuminated a small circle of ground about a foot in front of me.

Great.

I stumbled down the road like a drunken bum, wishing more than anything that I had on army boots instead of Dollar Store shower shoes. I tripped over a stick in the road and blew out my left shoe.

Awesome.

As I limped along in the dark on one flip-flop, I wondered, *did that make me a flip or a flop?*

Heavy rustling in the bushes to my left made me forget all about my lack of proper footwear.

I squelched a scream and took off running for all I was worth. By the time I reached the end of the lane and saw the dim light emanating from the front window of Winky's RV, I was as barefoot and out of breath as my cousin Tammy Jeeter that time I caught her behind the barn with Tommy Knocksworth.

Panting alone in the dark, my breath sounded like an obscene phone call to myself. I crept up to the dilapidated RV and shone the pale, blue light around the front steps. My suitcase was still sitting beside the stairs expectantly, like a stood-up date.

I grabbed the handle and hauled it toward Maggie. My old Ford Falcon was just where I'd left her.

Yesterday, I'd loosened the duct tape holding the tarp down on Maggie's driver's side. The wind must have blown the tarp up and over. It was folded away from the driver's seat, but still covered the passenger side. I took a limping step toward the right side of the car to un-tape the other half of the tarp.

Suddenly, four flashlights flicked on around me like humongous lightning bugs. Above each one, the outline of a hillbilly's face was caught in the surrounding, yellowish glow.

"Where you think you're goin'?" Slim asked.

In one synchronized motion, he, Stumpy, Elmira and Charlene took a step toward me, tightening the gap between us like mullet net.

Oh, crap! Now what?

"Let's get the witch!" Elmira howled.

The four took another step forward. I took one back...and stepped on something.

I looked down and my heart thumped. It was the makeshift broom-crutch thing Goober had made for me. I snatched it up, plastered on my best evil sneer, and shook it at them.

"Get out of here!" I screeched. "Leave me be, or I'll cast an evil spell on the lot of you!"

To my utter amazement, they scattered like a pile of rednecks being chased by Bigfoot.

"Huh," I muttered in astonishment. I turned around. Bigfoot was standing two feet away from me.

Suddenly, the earth came up and hit me in the face.

WHEN I CAME TO, BIGFOOT had me in his arms, toting me toward Winky's RV.

"Let me go!" I screeched, and wrestled with the hairy beast.

"For cripes sake!" Bigfoot said.

"You can talk?" I asked, incredulous.

"Val, it's *me*."

"Goober?"

"Who else?"

"Well, why didn't you say so?"

He set me down and laughed. "I guess I didn't want to ruin it for the others."

"I suppose this means going back to Walmart is out of the question," I said, and fished around in my purse for the keys to Maggie.

"Yes," Goober answered. "I'll meet you at the main road."

"Where can we go?" I asked as I tossed my suitcase and duffle bag in the backseat and opened the driver's side door.

"I've got an idea. Just follow me." Goober waved and took off jogging down the dirt lane.

Great. Now I'm taking advice from Sasquatch.

I thought about going back inside the RV for my baloney, but I heard muffled voices. I looked down the road in the other direction and saw four flashlight beams heading my way.

Not again!

I scrambled into the driver's seat and smooshed the tarp away that still enveloped half of Maggie. I cranked the engine to life, shifted into reverse, and backed up into the dirt lane.

The sound of Maggie's muffler must have stirred up the mob. In the rearview mirror, I could see the lights were bobbing up and down now, drawing nearer by the second.

Time to make like a tree and leaf....

I punched the gas. Maggie's glasspacks roared and echoed off the nearby aluminum abodes. Her tires kicked up an orange cloud of sand, and she fishtailed down the narrow, sandy lane.

A few seconds later, the lights behind me were getting smaller.

I sucked in a sigh of relief and reached to adjust the rearview mirror for a better view. My hand hit something swinging from it. I nearly pissed my panties. It was that horrible shrunken head, come to get me again!

I swatted at the hideous thing and lost control of Maggie. She veered into the overgrowth of bushes. A long, metallic scraping sound set my teeth on edge.

Oh, crap on a cracker!

"Sorry, Maggie."

I wrestled with the steering wheel until I got her centered back on-to the narrow road. I punched the gas.

As I cleared the exit to the Hell'ammo, Maggie's headlights lit up the side of Goober's old RV. He had the Minnie Winnie back on the road and ready to roll.

Goober waved a hairy arm and took off like a chimp who'd just heisted a banana wagon. I punched the gas and followed him in hot pursuit.

Right about the time I hit seventy miles an hour, the duct tape on the front passenger side of the car let loose. The silver tarp flew up alongside the car like a ghost. But the tape on the rear panel held tight. The tarp started flapping behind Maggie like a cape.

A thrill shot through me like a bolt of lightning. I looked up at the night sky full of stars and laughed like a madwoman.

Look out, world! Here comes the Redneck Avenger!

SOMEWHERE BEFORE WE hit the main road, the silver tarp came loose in the back and tumbled down the road behind me into the dark-ness like a dead body in an ill-fitting spacesuit.

I followed Goober right onto SR 60. It wasn't long before he turned off and pulled into the last place I would have ever expected.

The Polk County Police Station.

I pulled Maggie up alongside the RV.

"You've got to be kidding," I said as Goober poked his unmasked head out the window.

"Where else could we be safer?" he asked.

I sighed. "I guess you've got a point there. And I'm way too tired to argue."

"Finally, my lucky day."

"Hardy har-har."

Goober took his hairy Bigfoot hands off the steering wheel and grinned. His gold tooth shone in the moonlight like a bad toothpaste commercial.

"You look like a wreck, Val. I sure hope you've got the energy to take a shower before you hit the sack."

"Hey, you're the one impersonating a skunk ape."

Goober shook his bald head.

"I beg to differ."

Chapter Thirty-Two

"Aww, crap! My phone didn't charge," I said as I stumbled out of the tiny bedroom toward the smell of brewing coffee.

Goober was in the kitchen, shirtless, pouring himself a cup. He turned around to face me and my jaw went slack. Goober had two navels!

"What the...?" I asked.

Goober's smile evaporated. A hand flew down to cover his midsection. "Sorry. I got shot once. Left a terrible scar."

"Oh. I...I didn't know. How did it happen?"

"I'd rather not say. And Val? Don't say a word to anyone, okay?"

"Geez, Goober. At this rate, I won't even be able to claim I ever knew you."

Goober grinned. "That's o—"

The thunderous sound of a megaphone pierced the air. Someone bellowed, "Come out with your hands up."

Goober and I looked at each other.

"Not again."

"At least you got to have a sip of coffee first," I whined.

From between the blinds, I could see Chief Collins standing in the lot. He looked pretty pissed for 7:30 in the morning.

"Wait a minute," I said to Goober as he reached for a shirt. "Is this about Woggles...or *you?*"

Goober sighed and slipped the t-shirt on over his head.

"I guess we'll find out soon enough."

WE STEPPED OUT OF THE RV with our hands up. Chief Collins blew a whistle, and he and five other cops burst out laughing.

Neither Goober nor I got the joke.

"Mornin', you two!" Chief Collins said. "We were just havin' some fun. Come on in for some coffee and donuts. We got a confession out of Elmira last night. She called up and told us she did it."

"I had a feeling," I said as I stumbled toward the Chief, still undecided whether I was peeved at him or relieved. "How'd she do it?"

Chief Collins patted me on the back. "Crushed up apple seeds and put 'em in old Woggles' Geritol. She made craft stuff with apples, you know. Saved up the seeds."

"I know," I said. "Wait a minute!" I ran over to Maggie and snatched the shrunken head from the rearview mirror. "She made *this*, didn't she?"

"Yep, I'd imagine," Chief Collins said as he studied the head. He sniffed it. "Made from a dried-up apple, all right."

"What was her motive?" Goober asked.

"Had a life insurance policy out on him," Chief Collins explained. "Elmira told me, and I'm paraphrasing here, 'As old Woggles showed no signs of dying of his own accord, I decided to take it upon myself to speed up the process.'"

"You don't say," Goober said, shaking his head.

As we entered the station, Detective Rogers stepped up with his clipboard.

"Coroner's report confirms it Chief. The dumpster raccoon and Mr. Walters were both poisoned with the same agent."

"What does that mean?" I asked.

Chief Collins smiled. "It means you're both free to go."

AFTER FINISHING OFF two cups of coffee and three donuts each, Goober and I said our adieus to the Polk County Police Department.

"Can you believe that?" I asked as we stepped out into the parking lot. "Elmira killed him with apple seeds."

I studied the shriveled head in my hand. For the first time I noticed the slits that made up its cat-like pupils were actually deadly apple seeds.

"Sure," Goober said. "Apple seeds contain amygdalin. When you ingest them, it releases cyanide."

The harmless shriveled head in my hand suddenly regained some of its voodoo power. I held it a little further from me.

"So, why don't people die from eating apple cores, then?"

Goober looked up in the sky, as if searching for something.

"You'd need, I'd say, about a hundred and fifty seeds to kill someone the size of Woggles."

I eyed Goober with a mixture of trepidation and respect. "How do you *know* that?"

Goober shrugged. "Sorry. That's part of my 'Don't ask, don't tell,' policy."

"Argh!"

I flung the shrunken head into Maggie's backseat.

"Okay. But Goober, what if you ate fewer seeds? Like maybe fifty or something?"

Goober's lips twitched to one side.

"I suppose that'd be enough to cause dizziness and nausea. Maybe a bit of brain damage. Possibly impotency."

"Geez. I wonder. Do you think Elmira's been poisoning anybody else at the Hell'ammo?"

Goober snorted. "Who knows? I mean, with that crowd, how could you tell?"

I smiled. "Right. I guess we should get going."

"Okay. You want to follow me back, Val?"

"No. Don't worry. I know my way home from here."

Goober smiled softly. "I believe you do. Hold on a minute."

He climbed inside the RV and came out holding my cellphone.

"I'm afraid it didn't charge up much. Use your one phone call wisely."

"I will. See you back in St. Pete."

"Okay." Goober hesitated. "How about a hug?"

"Uh...sure."

I hugged Goober tight, then watched as he climbed into the old Minnie Winnie and rattled off out of the parking lot. As he disappeared down SR 60, I clicked on my phone and saw a voicemail from Tom. I played it.

"Val? Are you all right? I can't find you. I'm worried sick!"

My heart flinched.

Why is Tom so worried? I told him I was with Goober.

"Val," Tom's voice continued, "I have to tell you something about Goober. Call me back, please!"

My gut sank to my knees. I clicked speed dial for Tom. He answered on the first ring.

"Val! Are you okay?"

"Yes, I'm fine. Don't worry. I've been cleared of all charges."

I waited for him to say more, but he didn't. I looked at my phone. It had blacked out. The battery was dead.

Crap!

I slipped the phone into my purse and climbed into Maggie's driver's seat. I cranked the engine, shifted into reverse, and began to back out of the slot.

Suddenly, a pinched face shrouded in toilet-paper tubes was standing beside the car.

"Mornin' Val," Charlene said. She looked guiltier than a member of Weight Watchers nabbed at an all-you-can-eat barbeque.

"I'm sorry about accusing you of killin' Woggles," Charlene confessed. "Turns out it was my own sister givin' Woggles them apples. All the while he thought they was healthy, she was poisonin' him! Shame on Elmira! Woggles was the best man there ever was. And she killed him! What am I supposed to do now?"

"I don't know," I said. "But take my advice."

"What's that?"

"Don't eat or drink anything she might offer you."

Charlene nodded, and I pulled out of the lot. As I turned onto SR 60, she climbed back onto her shopper chopper and waved.

I waved back.

Chapter Thirty-Three

On the drive back to St. Petersburg, I kept thinking about Goober and hoping I'd catch sight of the old RV rumbling west down I-275. I never did.

What did Tom want to tell me about him? He wasn't dying, was he? I thought about the hug he'd planted on me as we parted, and shivered in the ninety-four degree heat.

As I crossed the Howard Frankland Bridge back into Pinellas County, my thoughts turned to Elmira. I wondered if they'd apprehended her already, and if she was sitting on the cot in my old holding cell this very moment.

Before I knew it, I pulled up to my little, flat-roofed nothing of a house. It shone like a palace in my eyes. When Tom came bursting out the front door, it felt like the sweetest home there ever was.

"Val!" Tom yelled as I shifted into park. "You're okay!"

"Yes, of course," I said, unfastening my seat belt. "I told you so over the phone. I've been cleared of all charges."

Tom opened my car door and pulled me out. He squeezed me tightly to his chest.

"That wasn't what I was worried about. When we were talking, your phone cut out...I thought...Goober...."

I pushed back from Tom's embrace.

"What's happened to Goober? Is he all right?"

The fading worry in Tom's eyes resurged.

"Is *he* all right? Val, when I couldn't reach you or Goober, I tried to do a background search on him. He didn't come up on any database we searched. Val, there's no such person as Gerald Jonohhovitz!"

"That can't be right, Tom. Maybe you just spelled his name wrong. It's a mouthful, you know."

Tom's face registered a hint of relief.

"You're probably right. Anyway, it doesn't matter now. You're home. You're safe. I missed you, you know."

I grinned. "I can tell. I missed you, too."

"Welcome home," Tom whispered, and planted a kiss on my lips. "Here, let me grab your luggage."

He leaned over Maggie's frame, reached in the backseat and pulled out my suitcase.

"What's this?" he asked. Tom was holding Goober's redneck dreamcatcher up in the air for the whole neighborhood to see.

Goober!

I snatched it out of Tom's hands. "A bad joke."

I grabbed my purse from the passenger seat and hid the dream-catcher behind it as best I could as I made for the front door. A sudden thought, however, made me stop and turn around.

"Hey, Tom, can a raccoon die from eating apples?"

Tom looked up from examining the side of Maggie.

"I dunno. Geez, Val, that's a nasty scrape."

"I know. Tom, the whole ride home, I kept thinking about how Woggles died. Something doesn't seem right. I hate to say it..."

I looked over toward Laverne's house, then walked back to the car and lowered my voice. "But I'm not convinced Elmira did it. I don't want to see an innocent woman take the fall for killing Woggles if it was...Laverne's cookies that did—"

"Val!" Tom interjected. "Bad cooking never actually killed any-one...no one that I know of, anyway. Let's wait for the coroner's report before we jump to any conclusions, okay?"

"But that's just it, Tom. The report's already come in."

Tom stepped around to the back of Maggie. "What did it say?"

"That whatever killed that raccoon in the dumpster killed Woggles, too."

"So what's the problem?"

"I dunno. I just...hey, what are you doing?"

"Opening the trunk."

"There's nothing in there."

The trunk popped open. Tom grimaced. "That's not entirely true."

"What are you talking about?"

"Come see for yourself."

I walked over and stared inside the trunk. A dead raccoon stared back.

"THANKS FOR GETTING that thing out of my trunk, Tom," I said as I hauled my suitcase into the garage.

"No problem. That's what men are for," he quipped and wrapped a twist-tie around a garbage bag containing the dead raccoon.

"How in the world do you think it got in there?"

I dumped my clothes directly from the suitcase into the washing machine.

"Most likely through that rust hole in the undercarriage I told you to get it fixed. It probably died of asphyxiation from the fumes."

I turned on the washer. Tom followed me back inside and into the kitchen.

"But why wouldn't it have just crawled back out?"

"Well, that's hard to do when some maniac is driving eighty miles an hour."

"I never go past seventy-nine."

"*Right.* It was motion sickness that did him in."

"Huh. Maybe *that's* the reason."

I cracked open the fridge.

"The reason for what?"

Tom plunked down on a stool.

"For why the raccoon didn't leave, Tom. Maybe it was too sick to get out, so it died in there."

"Were Laverne's cookies in the trunk?"

I shot him some side eye and reached for a bottle of beer.

"No. But seriously, Tom. That first night I was at the Hell'ammo—"

"The *what?*"

I winced. "Uh...beer?"

"Sure."

I handed Tom a bottle. "Shell Hammock is uh...a long story. I'll tell you later. The point is, what I'm trying to say is that raccoons got in my car and ate Laverne's cookies. The next morning, I saw a sick raccoon stumbling around outside the RV. Do you think her cookies could have, you know, killed them?"

I popped the top on my beer and handed Tom the opener.

"There's only one way to find out."

I smiled hopefully. "So, you'll get your guys at work to test the raccoon?"

Tom raised his bottle of beer in a mock toast.

"Anything for you, Val."

"Thanks, Tom."

I took a slug of beer, then set the bottle on the counter and wrapped my arms around him.

"You know how much I love it when you use your cop powers for good."

"Yeah, right," he laughed. "You just can't resist a man in uniform."

"Maybe," I said. "But actually, I like *you* better *out* of uniform."

Tom set his beer on the counter next to mine.

"Well, Ms. Fremden, that can be arranged."

"DID YOU GET ANY WRITING done?" Tom asked as he leaned on the doorframe to the bedroom.

For once, the question didn't cause my upper lip to twitch with annoyance. I stretched my legs, shuffled my torso to sitting, and fluffed the pillows behind me.

"Yes, as a matter of fact, I did."

"Well, in that case, my girl deserves a cappuccino in bed."

"Mmmm," I hummed as I took the frothy-topped cup from his hand.

"Well, it might be crude, but it works," Tom said as he slid into bed beside me.

"What are you talking about?"

Tom shot me one of his boyish grins and pointed a finger toward the ceiling. I looked up. Hanging from the curtain rod above the headboard was a pair of pink panties and three dangling tin cans.

I laughed until I'd sloshed every drop of cappuccino from my warm, ceramic cup.

Chapter Thirty-Four

Two days had passed since my return. I was in my new home office Monday morning, pecking away at my computer when the doorbell rang. My retired Vegas-performing neighbor had detected my return.

"Hey, honey!" Laverne said when I opened the front door. "You're back early! How was your trip?"

"Okay. I managed to escape with my life. And I wrote my first short story."

Laverne grinned. "Can't ask for more than that now, can you? What's it called?"

"*The Snicker...*"

Oh crap! I can't tell Laverne that I'm using her cookies to murder someone!

"Uh...*The Snicker Bar Murders.*"

"That sounds great! Are you writing now, sugar?"

"Uh...yes."

"Well don't let me stop the budding author! I just happened to see that horrible scrape on poor Maggie, and wanted to make sure you're all right."

"I'm fine, thanks. But I'm afraid Maggie's a little worse for wear."

"If you don't mind, let me have a crack at covering that scratch."

"What? Really?"

"I was a nail technician in another life."

I shook my head and smiled.

"Well that sounds like a story in and of itself."

Laverne showed me her dentures. "You better believe it, honey!"

"Well, okay, then. Sure. Give it a go. Oh. Are you still going to cooking class on Thursday night?"

"Of course!"

"Okay then. Just pop over when you're ready to roll."

"Thanks. Will do. And Val?"

"Yeah?"

"It's good to have you back." Laverne reached her flabby spider arms out for a hug. I gave her one.

"It's good to be back."

THE BAD NEWS WAS, I hadn't lasted a week at the Hell'ammo. The good news was, it had proven to be just the inspiration I'd been searching for.

Over the past three days, I'd typed my fingers to the bone. I'd missed last week's class on *Mystery Writing for Fun and Profit*, but I'd more than made up for it. I had my assignments up to date, including a short story...actually, a couple of stories...to share with Mrs. Langsbury and the others at class tonight.

I was flying high.

But when I walked into the class, old lady Langsbury wasn't happy to see me. Her pursed lips were white. The rest of her face, usually translucent, had taken on the shade of a ripe pomegranate.

I slunk into a seat next to Victoria the librarian impersonator. She glared at me through her thick, Woody Allen glasses while red-headed Clarice crinkled her long, pinched nose and sniffed like I might have just farted.

"Well, I suppose we should get started," Langsbury said sourly.

"But Ms. Langsbury, shouldn't we wait for Judy and...that young guy?" I asked.

For some reason, I'd felt the need to raise my hand. I lowered it lamely.

"Jeff. They won't be returning to class."

"What? Why not?"

Clarice and Victoria sniggered until Langsbury's Medusa impression turned them to stone.

"Apparently, Ms. Bloomers has an apt name. She seems to be in the habit of losing hers."

"What?" I asked.

"Judy took the 'fun and profit' part of this class a little too literally."

"I'm sorry. I still don't get it," I said apologetically.

Langsbury blew out a breath and took a seat on the front edge of her desk.

"After hitting us all up for our potential as real-estate clients, Judy hit gold with Jeff. According to him, Judy showed Jeff and his father a couple of condos, then ran off with his dear old dad. Jeff called me this afternoon to let me know he'd just gotten word his father and Judy were shacking up together in the Bahamas."

Holy mackerel!

"So, did any of the three of you remaining manage to complete last week's assignment?" Langsbury asked.

"I did," I offered.

"Good. I could use a good laugh."

AFTER CLASS, LAVERNE approached Maggie with her latest deadly weapon in tow. A fresh batch of lemon bars.

"Is that your latest class project?" I asked as she climbed into the passenger's seat.

"Yeah. You want one?"

"Uh...no thanks. I'm on this new diet. No food after 6:00 p.m."

"All right."

Laverne put the plate on the floorboard and buckled herself in.

"I'm planning on taking these over to Winky's tomorrow, anyway. It'll be nice to see the whole gang together again, don't you think?"

"Yeah, it will. I hope it's more fun than my writer's group was tonight."

Laverne shot me a sideways glance with those pug eyes of hers. "What happened?"

I shifted into reverse and pulled out of the parking space.

"You remember that young man who was part of our hen party?"

"Yeah."

"Seems Judy Bloomers ran off with his dad after showing him some condos."

Laverne shook her horsey head. "Wonders never cease."

I turned onto First Avenue North and headed toward the beach.

"Yeah. The other ladies were pretty pissed about it. Judy flew the coop, and ruffled everybody else's feathers in the process."

"Those old biddies. They were probably mad because they didn't think of it first."

I laughed. "Could be. Speaking of men, how are things with you and J.D.?"

"I asked him to move out while you were gone."

I hit the brakes a little hard at a yellow light. "Oh. I'm sorry, Laverne!"

"Don't be. I'm not."

"What happened...if you don't mind me asking?"

Laverne smiled softly. "I got no secrets from you, Val. It was nothing terrible. J.D. just reminded me of the ins and outs of having a man around. I like my life the way it is."

"So, you two are through?"

"I wouldn't go that far. Like I've told you before. J.D. is just too...I dunno. *Stiff*. He's always doing everything so prim and proper. It's kind of dull, you know? I told him I like to have fun. Be spontaneous. Life's too short to live by others' rules and expectations, don't you think?"

"Sure."

"Besides, I'm okay without a man. I think J.D. and I work best as friends...with the occasional 'benefits' thrown in."

I looked over at the old lady who had to be pushing eighty.

"Good for you."

Laverne smiled. "Yeah. It is."

She motioned toward the platter of lemon bars. "You sure I can't tempt you with one?"

"Yeah. I'm sure."

Chapter Thirty-Five

It had been a great morning so far. I hadn't spilled my cappuccino or snapped the thick, red rubber band hanging around my wrist. Instead, I'd written nine-hundred and ninety-eight words in a new short story called *Golden Years*. I typed in "jellybean time," to round out my thousand-word count, and reached into the jar to collect my reward.

The phone rang. My roommate was on the line.

"Hey, Tom."

"You got those lemon bars made yet?"

"I'm working on it. I just wanted to get my word count in first. Just finished."

"Good. I'm proud of you. But don't forget about the lemon bars. I just got the toxicology report. That raccoon in your trunk was loaded with rat poison."

"Geez! Rat poison!"

"Val, you don't think Laverne could have mistaken it for baking powder, or something?"

"I have no idea, Tom. But...I'll do my best to find out."

"Meantime, I'll call Chief Collins."

"No. Let me, Tom. If you don't mind, I'd like to do it myself."

"Be my guest, Valliant Stranger, P.I."

"Don't be a jerk."

"I'm not kidding. You earned it. You're saving an innocent woman."

"And possibly convicting a friend."

"Maybe. Maybe not. Life can be full of tough choices."

I glanced over at the new daybed in my office. I hoped I'd never feel the need to use it.

"Right. Let's hope it doesn't come to that."

"WELL, HOWDY THERE, Ms. Fremden."

"Hi, Chief Collins."

"What can I do for you?"

"Well, I'm calling because I think I know what happened to Woggles."

"He was poisoned."

"Right. But I don't think Elmira did it."

The line was silent for a moment. "You don't say."

"Chief, you see, I had this feeling...that is, something kept bugging me about the raccoons."

"Let me put your mind at ease, Ms. Fremden. The varmints didn't drown Woggles. His lungs had no trace of water in them."

"No, that's not what I meant. You see, I saw a sick raccoon the day before Woggles was found dead. And when I got home, I found a dead raccoon in my trunk."

"My condolences to your family."

I sighed. "I'm serious, Chief. I had the police here test it. It was poisoned, too."

"I think we established that already."

"Yes. But it wasn't poisoned by apple seeds. When you ingest them, it turns into cyanide, or something like that."

"Yes, I'm aware of that."

"Woggles trapped raccoons for their skins to make hats and stuff."

"Ms. Fremden, we've already gone over this. Is there a point to all this?"

"Yes. Please just bear with me just a moment longer. The first night I was at the Hell...*Shell Hammock*, raccoons got into my car and ate some of the cookies I'd brought with me. Woggles must have chased them off and took the rest back to his place."

"So you think the poison that killed him was in the cookies you brought? Be careful. You're treading on thin ice...."

"Yes and no. I think that night Woggles was out baiting traps...putting rat poison out for the raccoons. The raccoon I found in my trunk was loaded with it. My theory is, Woggles saw the coons in my car and chased them away. While he was doing that, the poison he was using got onto the cookies. Either that or he didn't wash his hands very well after baiting the traps. He took the cookies home, ate them, and...well, you know the rest. I think through his own careless-ness, Woggles poisoned himself. Accidentally, of course."

"Well, that's an interesting theory. But Rogers already said the re-port showed that Elmira poisoned him."

"Not exactly, Chief. As I recall, Rogers said that Woggles and the raccoons died from 'the same agent.'"

"Hmmm. I believe you're right. 'Agent' could mean anything. Now why would Rogers say such a thing?"

"I don't know. I just don't want Elmira to go to jail for a crime she didn't commit."

"That's pretty nice of you, considering what went down between you two. She thinks you're a witch, you know."

"Yeah. I had a feeling."

Chief Collins laughed. "Who knows? Maybe you are. This idea of yours, if it had been true, would have been *magic* to her ears."

"What do you mean, *if it had been true?*"

"Well, you're not the only one who put on their thinking cap, Ms. Fremden. I got to ruminating over the whole thing myself, and decid-ed to peruse the coroner's report one more time. Turns out *nobody* poisoned Woggles. Not even himself. He didn't have a trace of anything in his system."

"But why did Detective Rogers—"

"Rogers confessed to me that he lied about the poison results. He was just trying to protect his best buddy Woggles from going down in history as an illegal poacher."

"But doesn't that mean that Rogers tried to frame Elmira?"

"I guess you could see it that way. But if we locked up everybody who made a mistake around here, there'd be nobody left to unlock the jail cells. And Miss Elmira wasn't totally innocent herself. She *did* try to poison Woggles. She just got lucky she's illiterate and can't count past thirty."

"But still..."

"Believe you me, Ms. Fremden, Detective Rogers isn't going unpunished. He's learning his lesson as we speak. Washing the inside of a dumpster is never any fun. Scrubbing every one within a mile of here in the stifling heat of summer makes it, as you can imagine, even more unpleasant."

"Country justice, Chief Collins?"

"*Poetic* justice, more like it."

"So then, Chief, if nobody poisoned Woggles, what *did* he die from?"

"Turns out, according to the coroner's report, Mr. Wallace Walters was a ripe *ninety-four* years old, Ms. Fremden. He died of old age."

"You don't say."

"Listen, I kept Elmira in the slammer for a week so she could ruminate on her evil ways. I'm releasing her as we speak. Hold on a second."

I heard the Chief's muffled voice over the speaker.

"Elmira, it's that Val Fremden lady. She called trying to clear your name. I think you owe her an apology."

"Chief!" I hollered into the phone. "That's not necessary!"

"Ms. Fremden, I just want to say thank you," Elmira's voice cracked over the phone. "I read you wrong. Seems like it's hard to know who to trust no more. That rascal Woggles told me he was seventy-four. Soon as I get home, I'm gonna shut down my profile on MatchMate. The internet ain't nothin' but a pack of lies!"

I stifled a laugh. "I couldn't agree with you more, Elmira. I wish the best of luck to you and your sister Charlene."

"Thanky."

Chief Collins took the phone. "Well, I guess that about sums it up, Ms. Fremden."

"I'd say so. Thanks for giving me the benefit of the doubt, Chief Collins."

"I find it almost always pays to do so. Take care, young lady."

"You too, Chief."

I clicked off the phone.

Poor Woggles. His last meal was Laverne's cookies. No matter what, that was a crummy way to go.

I heard the familiar sound of Tom's SUV pulling up in the driveway. I'd never been so glad to be in a relationship in all my life. I ran to the door and opened it.

"Hi, there. I'm glad you're home."

Tom grinned. "I'm glad to be home. Home with you, that is."

I gave Tom a kiss to build a dream on.

"Dang. Too bad we've got a prior engagement."

"I know. But you've got a raincheck. Get changed while I call Laverne. Chez Winky awaits."

Chapter Thirty-Six

Laverne's stork legs picked their way across the strip of lawn between our houses. In her hands rested a batch of lemon bars set to launch a thousand trips to the toilet. But, I suppose, that was better than to the grave.

"Let me get those for you," Tom said.

He took the plate from Laverne and handed it over to me like it was a ticking time bomb. He spoke more for Laverne's benefit than mine.

"Here, take these, Val, while I get the door for Ms. Cowens."

Laverne beamed at both of us like a country porch light. As her strawberry-blonde curls ducked into the SUV, I pitched her tray of lemon bars into the bushes and picked up a double batch I had ready and waiting in the driveway at my feet.

"All tucked in?" I asked. It was Tom's and my secret code for "All's clear."

"Yes," Tom said and winked. "I'll put those in the back."

"Y'all take such good care of me," Laverne said as I handed Tom the counterfeit lemon bars.

I climbed into the SUV.

"We take good care of each other, Laverne."

Laverne sighed and settled into her seat.

"That's the way a family should be."

AS WE PULLED UP IN front of Winky and Winnie's shiny new dou-blewide, a streak of redneck pride straightened my shoulders and made my lips curl upward. But when the door flew open and Winky blustered out to welcome us in, I had to fight back a tear.

Family isn't who birthed you or raised you, so much as who you care about, and who cares about you.

"Y'all come on in!" Winky beamed, and hugged Winnie to his barrel chest. "Show 'em, honeybuns."

Winnie held out her hand. It was surprising she could lift it, given the size of the rock on her finger.

"We're engaged!" she gushed, and adjusted the red glasses on her pudgy, button nose.

"Congratulations!" Tom and Laverne hollered.

"It's about time," I said, and elbowed Winky in the ribs.

Winky stuck his tongue out at me.

"And we got us some more good news."

He handed me a newspaper.

"Looky here. The Donut Shack done got writ up in the *Sunset Beach Busy Bee.*"

"Not for code violations, I hope," Tom quipped.

"Nice one, Tom," I said, genuinely impressed. "You're getting better with the jokes."

Tom waggled his blond eyebrows at me. "See, you *can* teach an old dog new tricks."

"Speakin' a dogs, Milly says the pups will be ready to go next week," Winky said.

"Where *is* Milly?" I asked. "I saw her Beemer out front."

"Back in the movie room with Vance," Winnie said. "Follow me."

"Hold on a second."

I stuck a hand in my purse and pulled out something.

"Winky, this is for you. A little thanks for letting me stay at your place in Shell Hammock."

Winky's jaw dropped. "It must 'a cost you a fortune!"

"Not really," I said, and handed him the plastic Dale Earnhardt cup I'd found in a pile of debris at the Hell'ammo.

"Woo hoo!"

Winky held the cup up like he'd just won a solid-gold trophy.

"Now my NASCAR Big-Gulp collection is a hunnert percent complete!"

Winnie shook her head and smirked. "How can I ever thank you, Val?"

"Sorry."

"No, I'm serious. Now maybe he'll get off eBay and do some work around here. How was it at Shell Hammock?"

"To be honest, I never dreamed I'd end up having another chance to be the young chick driving all the old men crazy."

"I heard you got yourself in a bit a trouble over there," Winky said.

"Just jail, and only once," I shrugged. "Followed by house arrest."

Winky grinned. "That's the good thing about livin' in a trailer, y'all. If'n you're on house arrest, you can still make a beer run. Just hook yore trailer to yore pick-em-up truck and go."

Tom shook his head. "I think you might want to review the statutes, Winky."

"What fer? I ain't got none yet. Less'n you count the gnome Laverne give us last time y'all was here."

I SET THE LEMON BARS down on the kitchen counter and followed Winnie into the sunken living room while the guys and Laverne went out back to fire up the barbeque grill. Laverne always did prefer a flickering light show....

Nacho Libre was playing on the screen in the fancy, sunken media room. Jorge, Sherryl, Milly and Vance sat there like drugged zombies.

Each had been lulled into wanton complacency by alcohol and the dual-action, massage options on their Barcaloungers.

Jorge's eyes sparked back to life when he saw me.

"Hey, Val."

Sherryl weakly waved a manicured hand.

"Who's turn is it to take down Laverne's cooking?" Jorge asked. "What did she bring?"

"Lemon bars," I said.

"Oh no!" Winnie cried out behind me.

She held a slightly used lemon bar between her pinched fingers like a dead rat.

"I already swallowed some of it!"

"Don't worry!" I said. "Those are mine. Tom and I did a bait-and-switch before we left. You're okay."

"Whew!" Winnie took another bite and mumbled, "These are delish, by the way."

"Should we join the others in the backyard?" I asked.

"Do we have to?" Milly moaned from her chair. "I think I could live the rest of my life in this thing."

"Who would take care of me and Charmine?" Vance asked.

Milly raised her head, then let it fall back on the headrest.

"Not my problem."

I WALKED OVER TO THE fire pit to find Winky busy grilling a bunch of hotdogs stuck on the tines of a rake.

"You've got to be kidding me," I said.

"I dare you to find a more efficient way a roastin' wieners," he replied. "Grab that rake with the marshmallows on it and we'll make us some s'mores."

Sherryl laughed. "I'll do it," she said, and took the rake.

"Here, Val," Winky said. "These here wieners are done. Hold the handle while I pull 'em off and reload."

"So, what are you going to name your new puppy?" Sherryl asked.

"Pigmailman," Winky said.

"You mean Pygmalion? The mythical king?" Sherryl asked.

"No. After the mailman," Winky said. "He's fat as a hog."

"How about you, Val?"

"I don't know yet. You?"

"We were thinking of Lady," Jorge said as he walked up with two beers. He handed one to Sherryl.

"What do you think of the name, Val?" Sherryl asked. She turned the rake to toast the marshmallows on the other side.

"I dunno. Lady? I never met a dog who lived up to that name."

Winky laughed. "I know that's right."

He finished sliding a new round of hotdogs onto the tines.

"Jorge, take charge of this while I prepare the seafood."

Jorge took the rake laden with wieners and stood next to Sherryl. Winky began slicing through the hotdogs, three-quarters up the long way.

"What are you doing, Winky?" I asked.

He picked up one of the finished wieners. Six leg-like appendages curled outward from the intact end, making the hotdog look like a slightly charred octopus.

"That's gross," I said.

Winky looked at the octo-dog and shrugged.

"I thought you liked seafood, Val."

"IT'S TOO BAD COLD CUTS and Bill couldn't make it," Milly said as we bobbed around in the pool with our stomachs full to the bursting point.

"I know," Tom said. "The whole gang would be here."

"Wait a minute," Laverne said. "What about Goober? Where's he?"

"I haven't seen him," Jorge said.

"Isn't he staying with you guys?" Vance asked.

"Not anymore. He moved out about a week ago. I went into his room and it was cleared out. It looked like he left in a hurry, too. He didn't even take his terrarium."

"He left without his medication?" Winky asked.

"No," Jorge said. "*Terrarium*. The cage for his lizard."

"I didn't know he had a pet lizard," I said.

"Nobody did but me," Jorge said. "Goober never would let anyone in his room."

"I wondered what he was doing with those mealworms," Sherryl said. She turned to me and whispered, "But I didn't really want to know. You know what I mean?"

I nodded. "I do."

"A good man don't talk about his lizard in mixed company," Winky said.

Milly sighed. "He quit his job with me last week. I haven't heard from him since."

"Last time I saw him, he was heading back here in Cold Cuts' RV," I offered.

"Well, doesn't *anybody* know where he is?" Laverne asked.

"I'm right here!" yelled a voice from the yard.

A moment later, the steps to the redwood deck began to squeak. Suddenly, standing at the pool edge was a small, silver-haired man in a red speedo.

"Bombs away!" he said, and took a flying leap.

We watched, dumbfounded, as persnickety Mr. J.D. Fellows, Esq. drew his knees to his chest and cannon-balled into the pool.

The shockwave split the side of the pool, and before anybody knew what was happening, we all went washing across the lawn like a burst bag of dime-store goldfish.

Chapter Thirty-Seven

*S*ometimes, *the strangest things turn out to be true. But this isn't one of them.*

The End.

I sat back and smiled. Another short story done and dusted. Finally, I was doing something memorable with my life. And thanks to the rubber band around my wrist, it was looking more and more unlikely that I would end up being buried in a piano case.

To top it off, Chief Collins had shared my story with the editor of *The Polk County Poker.* They wanted to publish *The Snickerdoodle Murders* in their Sunday short-story section!

Maybe I won't end up in the gutter eating cat food after all....

I took a jelly bean from the jar and stood up for a stretch. The postman's jeep passed by on the street. I glanced at the time on my phone. Geez! It was already past two o'clock!

I braved the heat of midday and sprinted to the mailbox. Inside was a small package wrapped in brown paper.

I opened it and nearly screamed.

Inside was a pair of shrunken heads and a note scrawled in red ink. It read; *To Val, with our thanks, Elmira and Charlene.*

I shook my head in wonder at the sheer, hideous waste of two perfectly good apples. I reached to close the lid on the mailbox, but something else inside caught my eye.

I thrust my hand in and pulled out a postcard postmarked Greenville, Florida. I thought at first it was from my adoptive mom, Lucille Jolly. But that was highly unlikely. Whoever sent it had wished me well.

On the front side was a picture of a beautifully crafted dreamcatcher. Its beads and feathers glistened in the sun as it dangled from the ceiling of a quaint, country porch full of rocking chairs laden with comfy pillows.

I flipped the card back over and re-read the message. Whoever had written it hadn't signed their name. But I had a good idea who the sender was, just the same. I hoped he would return one day.

The sappy, pre-printed inscription on the postcard read: *I hope all your dreams come true.*

But scrawled in the message section were the words:

If you ever need me, you know how to catch me.

I held the postcard to my heart, swallowed the lump in my throat, and headed back inside my air-conditioned palace.

DEAR READER,

Thanks so much for reading Seven Daze! I hope you found the story up to snuff! Sorry, that's a real expression my grandparents used to use. My grandma loved her some Butternut snuff. If I close my eyes, I can still see the yellow label wrapped around the tin it came in....

You see, like Val, I'm half redneck, too.

I spent summers on a farm in North Florida, gathering chicken eggs, rolling watermelons down hills, and even riding a huge hog named Jason around in his pen. One day, Jason ran away. All of us kids were sad that he'd taken off, but we enjoyed the big slabs of bacon grandma started serving up with breakfast the next morning.

I was so naïve I was nearly forty before I figured out that I'd been hoodwinked. Poor Jason had gone to hog heaven. Still, he *was* delicious.

While I was writing Seven Daze, I actually made a booking to go to a trailer park in Polk County. One thing led to another and things didn't work out. But perhaps the story is better for it. Truth is stranger than fiction, and often times, not quite as funny.

And in case you're wondering, no. I've never seen Bigfoot.

If you'd like to know when my future novels come out, please subscribe to my newsletter. I won't sell your name or send too many notices to your inbox.

Newsletter Link: https://dl.bookfunnel.com/fuw7rbfx21

Thanks again for reading my book!

Sincerely,

Margaret Lashley

P.S. I live for reviews! The link to leave yours is right here:

https://www.amazon.com/dp/B07D6FGMPC#customerReviews

P.S.S. (Busted inner tube?) If you'd like to contact me, you can reach me by:

Website: https://www.margaretlashley.com

Email: contact@margaretlashley.com

Facebook: https://www.facebook.com/valandpalspage/

What's Next for Val?

Firest of All, Thanks for Reading Seven Daze!
I hope you enjoyed it! If you did, please take a moment and leave a review now. I appreciate every single one!

https://www.amazon.com/dp/B07GW4H956#customerReviews

Ready for more Val? Set your sights on *Figure Eight: Yardsale Karma*. As Val and Tom struggle to blend their households, one hideous intruder could spell doom for their relationship! It's funny how it's the simple things that can drive us crazy...

Click the link below to get *Figure Eight: Yardsale Karma* now!

https://www.amazon.com/dp/B07GW4H956

Here's a sample of what you're in for:

A Sneak Peek at Figure Eight:

Chapter One

During my half-century on this planet, I'd learned that *everybody* had some kind of secret stuffed away in their closet. Some folks called them skeletons. Others called them boogey men.

As for me, what hid away in *my* closet was made of ceramic.

And it compelled me to do it bodily harm.

"DO ME A FAVOR, VAL. Change your clothes."

My bleary eyes glanced up from the computer screen. I'd been pecking away at the keyboard since 3 a.m., when I'd been throttled awake by a crazy story idea that'd left my mind wobbling around in circles like a gerbil in a lopsided wheel.

Tom, my long-time boyfriend and short-time housemate, leaned against the door of my home office. Blond, clean-shaven, and in a cop uniform crisp enough to crunch, it almost appeared as if he'd been sent by the government to force me to clean up my act.

"Why should I change my clothes?" I argued.

"Because I almost mistook you for a homeless drifter," he said.

Both Tom and the frothy cup of cappuccino in his hand were two temptations I found hard to resist. Still, I always gave it my best shot.

"Nobody can see me, Tom. Besides...these are my...uh...*business pajamas.*"

Tom's left eyebrow ticked upward.

"There's no such thing as *business pajamas*, Val. Unless you're a 'lady of the night.' But *you*, my dear, could never be one of *those....*"

"Thank you." I smiled and batted my eyes demurely.

"....because we both know you can't stay awake past 9:30."

Tom drove his jab deeper with an exaggerated wink. My lips twisted into a sneer faster than a barefoot tourist in an asphalt parking lot.

"Hardy har har, Tom. You know, I think I liked you better when you couldn't tell a joke."

Tom pretended to be confused. "Who's joking?"

"Ugh!" I rolled my bloodshot eyes. "You win, okay? Now, hand over the cappuccino before somebody gets hurt."

Tom laughed, gave me the cup, and tousled my nappy bed-head as if I were a child. I took a greedy sip of the delicious brew and watched Tom fiddle with the shirt collar on his perfectly pressed police uniform.

"When you're done with the cappuccino, get a shower and get dressed, would you?" he said. "Go out and see the world. It's still out there, you know."

I scowled. "This never would have happened if I hadn't let you move in."

"What wouldn't?" Tom quipped. "You working at home, or your total abandonment of personal hygiene?"

I glared at Tom. "Like I said before, I liked you better when you couldn't tell a joke."

"And like *I* said, I'm not joking. I'm heading off to work now. Why don't you come up for air, Val...and give the rest of us a breather, too?"

"Another zinger," I deadpanned. "Maybe *you* should be a writer."

Tom shook his head.

"Nope. *One's* plenty enough for this place. I gotta go."

He handed me the morning paper, kissed me goodbye, and disappeared down the hallway. A moment later, I heard the front door close behind him.

I peeked out the blinds to make sure Tom was gone, then I sniffed my right armpit.

Good thing I was sitting down.

Okay. So I've been in my pajamas since Monday. Big deal. That was only two days ago.

I glanced down at the *St. Petersburg Times*. It must have been a typo. According to the paper, it was Thursday, July 18th.

"What?" I muttered.

Four days! Gone by in a blur!

I leaned back in my chair, tapped a finger on my desk, and vaguely recalled a string of hurried, takeout dinners with Tom, followed by typing into the night until I couldn't see straight, then falling into bed long after Tom was fast asleep.

My word count for the week was incredible. But my love life was definitely down for the count.

I sat up and sighed.

At least Angela Langsbury, my writing instructor, would be proud when I showed up to class tonight with my latest story. But if I didn't get a bath and return to the "planet of the washed" soon, Tom and I might soon be all washed-up.

I took another sip of cappuccino and looked down at my computer screen. My gerbil mind took a tentative step on its wobbly wheel.

I'll just finish this scene, and then I'll take a little break....

<u>Chapter Two</u>

The doorbell rang. My flying fingers froze and hovered above the keyboard. I glanced at the clock.

It's half-past noon!

I padded to the door and peeked out the peephole. Either I'd forgotten it was national Wear Every Piece of Jewelry You Own Day, or I was being paid a call by my next-door neighbor, Laverne Cowens.

I opened the door. Laverne let out a little gasp. Her eyes doubled in size, and the crescent of red lipstick below her nose melted like a Christmas candle in a microwave.

"Oh my word, honey! Have you been sick?"

"No," I said, and winced. The sunlight flashing off Laverne's sequined blouse was blinding. I crossed my arms and tucked my fingers under the armpits of my smelly gray t-shirt. "Why would you ask *that?*"

"Well, I haven't seen you for darn near a week...and you look like—"

"I've been *busy*," I said. "*Writing* and stuff, you know?"

"Oh." Laverne eyed me up and down. She didn't look that convinced.

I tapped my foot on the threshold. "Did you *need* something, Laverne?"

Her donkey-shaped head raised up until our eyes met again. She flashed her horsey dentures at me.

"No, honey. I just wanted to make sure you saw this."

Laverne poked a pink flyer at me.

"What is it?" I asked.

"Why, it's my favorite time of the year, Val. The annual neighborhood yard sale and bake-off!"

"Oh. Why didn't I get a flyer?"

"I dunno. I got mine Sunday."

I briefly scanned the flyer. My eyebrows shot up an inch. "Is this a typo? It says here that this year's bake-off winner has to *kiss a pig.*"

Laverne snorted. "I know! Isn't it fabulous? I've always wanted to do that!"

I looked at the skinny old woman sideways and, for a second, worried about the state of her mental health. Then I remembered that, given her baking skills, Laverne's prospects of winning the bake-off were as likely as that pig's were of sprouting wings and flying off to New Jersey.

"Are you gonna have a table and sell stuff this year?" Laverne asked.

As I mulled over the idea, my eyes wandered from the flyer and stared absently at the flashy gold sequins spelling out "I Love Vegas" on Laverne's shirt.

If I *did* participate, it would mark my first time doing so. Not because I didn't like a good yard sale, but because until now, I didn't have anything spare to sell.

When my life in Germany had collapsed five years ago, I'd been forced to whittle my belongings down to what fit inside two shabby suitcases. My first hovel of an apartment back in St. Pete had been furnished solely with the junk abandoned by its former occupant.

Then, a few years ago, I'd inherited this house.

Ironically, having been handed a house full of hoarder's junk had turned me into a minimalist. I'd thrown out pretty much everything in the place, and had furnished its empty hull sparsely—namely the same recycled full-size bed and side table that had come with my tiny apartment. To that I'd added a cheap cappuccino maker and a few assorted sheets and towels.

The day I'd moved into this house, I'd left the rest of the junk from the apartment, including a crappy old couch, in the alley by the dumpster. But later that same day, Tom had arrived, dragging that nasty old couch along with him as a sort of gag gift.

Unbeknownst to him, a hitchhiker in the form of a dead finger had come along for the ride. The derelict digit had given me a run for my money with the law, and a lingering fear of used upholstery that some might argue bordered on clinical neurosis.

I'd replaced the finger-infested couch, and, after many attempts to unload my boyfriend, had finally decided to keep him.

Living alone had enabled me to keep things at my house pretty well pared down to the basic necessities. But all that had changed a few weeks ago, when Tom moved in...and brought all *his stuff* along with him.

I handed the flyer back to Laverne.

"Well, are you?" she asked.

"Am I what?"

"Are you gonna have a table at the yard sale this year?"

A grin crawled across my lips like a fly stuck in honey.

"Yeah. I think I will. But Tom's not gonna like it."

Laverne opened her mouth to speak, but the sudden sound of hammering struck us both dumb. We turned and looked down my driveway. The hammering was coming from the residence that bordered the left side of my lawn.

Our new neighbor, Jake Johnson, was pounding a sign into his yard. Perspiration glistened from his bald head. It was late July, so I assumed the rest of him was drenched in sweat as well. But it was impossible to be sure. With the exception of the top of Jake's head, as far as I could tell his entire body was covered in thick, black hair.

The term "swarthy" didn't even *begin* to do Jake justice.

As I watched him beat on the sign post, I couldn't stop myself from wondering if maybe, just maybe, Jake Johnson was the Missing Link scientists had been searching for....

"Hi, Jake!" Laverne called out.

Jake looked over and waved. Short and muscular like an erect chimpanzee, he gave the sign post one more whack, then lumbered toward us, pounding the hammer in his fist as if he were practicing for his next target.

If Laverne had known everything *I* knew about our primitive neighbor, she'd have pirouetted on her gold high heels and fled for the hills.

A couple of months ago, Jake had been released from prison after serving twenty years for arson. And...uh...for barbequing his mother. According to newspaper reports, Jake had used a bedroom in his house next door as a kind of makeshift crematorium.

Most folks around here thought Jake was guilty as sin. But a few believed that his mother had been a victim of spontaneous combustion, and that he'd been wrongly convicted.

I was among those few.

Still, I had to admit, Jake had a rather worrisome penchant for outdoor grilling....

But whether Jake had been guilty or not, I would forever be indebted to him. During his time in the slammer, he'd earned a degree in pet psychology. Since his release, he'd put his new-found skills to work, helping skittish, incorrigible canine clients overcome their neuroses.

To non-believers, dog psychology may have sounded as preposterous as spontaneous combustion. But not to me. Not *anymore*, anyway. Not long ago, Jake's unorthodox "primal howl" treatment had cured me of my fear of wedding rings, thus enabling me to lead a more full and productive life.

A smile curled my lips. The memory of sitting around a fire, howling with a poodle in Jake's backyard warmed my heart. I waved at my therapist as he crossed the yard.

"Howdy, neighbor," I said.

Jake had barely gotten within arm's length of us when Laverne jabbed the pink flyer at him.

"You having a table this year?" she asked, wriggling as if her bladder were about to burst.

"I dunno. Don't got much to sell," Jake replied in an accent that reminded me the urban-dwelling ape-man once hailed from Jersey.

Hoboken-habilis.

Jake glanced to his left, then right, then pounded his fist palm with the hammer. As he looked me and Laverne up and down, I almost expected him to break out into a chimp mating call. But he lowered his gravelly voice and spoke in a half-whisper instead.

"You's guys, I think we got a thief in the 'hood. You know, that's the third sign I've put up this week. I get up in the morning, and, like, 'poof,' the sign's gone."

"What's it for?" Laverne asked. "The yard sale?"

"No. My animal therapy business."

"Huh. That's weird," I said.

"Animal therapy's not weird," Jake said defensively.

"No. I mean it's weird the signs are going missing," I said.

"So, you're not having a table, Jake?" Laverne whined, her face as fallen as a drop-kicked soufflé.

Jake shot me a quizzical look. I shrugged and mouthed the words, "Laverne loves yard sales."

Jake cleared his throat. "Well, hey, I can probably scrounge up a table. I mean, who ain't got junk? Or I'll *buy* something, for sure. You never know what you'll find at a yard sale."

Laverne's dentures beamed like pearly headlights. "That's right, Jake! That's the best part! Finding all the hidden treasures! Oh! I'm so excited I can hardly wait!"

"Yeah," Jake said, and looked at the flyer. "But I ain't too keen on this bake-sale thing."

My gut gurgled. I eyed Jake and shook my head ever so slightly. But it was too late.

"Why not?" Laverne asked. Her worried, pug eyes shifted back and forth between me and Jake.

"Personally, I think making a pig kiss a person qualifies as animal cruelty," Jake said.

Laverne put her hands on her hips and cocked her horsey head sideways.

"Well, now," she said, "I guess that would depend on what kind of person the pig had to kiss."

Click the link below to get *Figure Eight: Yardsale Karma* now! https://www.amazon.com/dp/B07GW4H956

About the Author

Like the characters in my novels, I haven't lead a life of wealth or luxury. In fact, as it stands now, I'm set to inherit a half-eaten jar of Cheez Whiz...if my siblings don't beat me to it.

During my illustrious career, I've been a roller-skating waitress, an actuarial assistant, an advertising copywriter, a real estate agent, a house flipper, an organic farmer, and a traveling vagabond/truth seeker. But no matter where I've gone or what I've done, I've always felt like a weirdo.

I've learned a heck of a lot in my life. But getting to know myself has been my greatest journey. Today, I know I'm smart. I'm direct. I'm jaded. I'm hopeful. I'm funny. I'm fierce. I'm a pushover. And I have a laugh that makes strangers come up and want to join in the fun. In other words, I'm a jumble of opposing talents and flaws and emotions. And it's all good.

In some ways, I'm a lot like Val Fremden. My books featuring Val are not autobiographical, but what comes out of her mouth was first formed in my mind, and sometimes the parallels are undeniable. I drink TNTs. I had a car like Shabby Maggie. And I've started my life over four times, driving away with whatever earthly possessions fit in my car. And, perhaps most importantly, I've learned that friends come from unexpected places.

Made in the USA
Columbia, SC
24 October 2022